Tea Time

Samantha Inman

BOULEVARD BOOKS
The New Face of Publishing
www.BoulevardBooks.org

ISBN 13 978-1-942500-55-1

TEA TIME

Prologue

They were sitting around a table on the porch of the family estate, waiting. She dressed in a casual blouse of light blue and mid-calf black skirt with her shoes next to her feet. Her hair was cut short to her shoulders with the beautiful wave to her dark hair. Her companion was sitting across the small table observing her exterior calm and patience. On the inside, it felt as though she was going to melt into a puddle. She hoped the nerves didn't show. Moving her right hand from the table as she realized her nails started to tap the patterned table runner. She held her hands, gripping her fingers in her lap and felt her toes gently tap. Her calm was cracking.

Her companion was in a pair of slacks, white starched buttoned shirt with a red tie and his jacket was hung over the back of the chair. His dark hair was shaped and combed to the side and his black framed glasses well fitted to his face surrounding his grey eyes. He was calm as ever, but behind those grey eyes was a cold viciousness she had seen weeks ago. The young housemaid came out with the tea and biscuits, with sugar, milk and jellies in these little painted china heirloom bowls, a matching tea pot, with silver and gold spoons on the aging silver tray.

"Thank you, Madeline," she said, politely with her beautiful accent.

"Is there anything else I can get you? " the seated woman shook her head no, "Yes, ma'am" she replied with a curtsey, then walked back into the house.

She then looked across the table and her face could be seen on the reflection of the glass table. She glanced for just a moment and realized how much like the photographs of her mother she resembled. Her father was a prominent member of Parliament and well-known English citizen and her mother, his first wife, was his friend and later assistant for many years before she became his wife. They had met on a trip had taken to visit his heritage homeland of Greece. She had been born in England but was visiting her family. It was like an old movie, the way they met. She was sipping a tea in a little café when her father was passing by and stopped. They talked for hours.

She died in childbirth with Adara, her second child. Her father remarried, not long thereafter, to a proper English woman of another prominent family: in fact, by all accounts they were in love and happily married despite the age gap. She was about ten years younger than Adara's father. She was still relatively young when they had a daughter, Mariana, her father's third child. James was the

3

eldest by five years, then Adara, and Mariana the youngest by ten years.

"Adara, what is this all about? " the young man asked.

She was distracted with the thoughts running through her mind, but still bristled at her full name "It's Ada," she let it sink in, then continued "Bill, I have to talk to you," Adara looked to the patio umbrella in an attempt to hold back the tears…of pain…or sadness, she wasn't sure. Breathing deep, letting the tears sting but refusing to let them fall, she managed to get the words out "I'm pregnant, and yes the child is yours." There was a slight bitterness to her voice. Adara had to say those words. Not truly knowing how he would react she stood up and walked towards the garden. Taking a handkerchief out of pocket in her skirt she wiped the tears before he could see her fear. With any other man she might have been able to let them fall, but not him. She did not hear Bill's footsteps as she put her hand to her abdomen.

"Ada, drink your tea before it becomes chilled." nudged Bill. He grabbed her wrist and she tried to pull away.

"Let go."

"Fine, but come back and finish, let's talk about this."

Adara walked back and added lemon, a small splash of cream and one cube of sugar to her tea and sipped, before sitting. She sipped once, twice more and began to feel drowsy. She put her hand to the table to steady the spinning. Adara closed her eyes after barely placing her teacup to the saucer before she slipped from her chair. The last sound she heard before slipping completely under the spell of the unknown drug was the wet sound of tea dripping onto the concrete patio floor.

The Pain

Chapter I

Present Day, Los Angeles, California,

9:05 am, Monday, April 27

Alena Martin awoke from a deep yet uneasy sleep as she heard the alarm on her cellphone. She had had the same nightmare for several weeks after her most recent case. She tapped the snooze button as she slowly stretches her aching body and moves the cover and sheets off of her body. She sits on the bed, feet touching the carpeted floor of the hotel room. She is dressed in a dark grey-tank top and a pair of purple pajama shorts. She tussles her red shaggy hair as she walks to the bathroom to take a shower. Alena looks into the small mirror and stares at her clear blue eyes and round face that has been round even after losing a significant amount of weight in her late teen years. She is perfectly average in height and weight with some muscle from years of training in a variety of childhood sports but hardly an ideal body of Hollywood.

Alena loved LA: the choked highways drowning in traffic, the heat kissing her skin no matter the season, the smell of the morning coffee slowing growing stale from the shop around the corner as it mingled with the cannabis smoke from the dispensary across the street. Despite the superficial and shallow exterior, there was more to this city. Alena loved every bit of it, even the occasional person filled with plastic and hope of everlasting youth.

Detective Alena Martin is in her late-twenties, yet considerably young to hold the office of detective in the Los Angeles police force. She was brilliant in her studies in college earning her degrees a year earlier than anticipated in Criminology and Forensic Anthropology and then decided to go into the police academy that year—she was 20 at the time. She again graduated with high regards. Her Captain at the time slowly groomed her to move up and Alena became a detective in Special Operations division in Robbery Homicide, five years ago. She was able to see and work with forensic understanding, psychological training and the experience gained over the past couple years. She was on her way to becoming a well-respected detective. She solved every case without fail and then came the Denton case. She shuddered as she lifted her tank top to just above her right hip, and she could see it. The mistake. The 9mm caliber bullet hole that knocked her on her ass, the scar became a scathing reminder that criminals have outwitted the police force with armor piercing bullets What shook her more wasn't the fact that it was the first time she was shot but that her first thought was *Well, shit I liked this shirt*. What came out of her mouth was "Shit, that's going to leave a mark." Her adrenaline pumped through her veins as she lifted her service weapon, aiming for his arm, and fired. She misfired and hit the gun in his hand, he dropped the weapon and ran out as her partner ran in. Her blood seeping through the shirt and flowing through her fingers as she applied pressure. Her knees had given way and she collapsed as the other officers ran in.

Gratefully, it did not kill her, but she thought, while on the ground that she was going to bleed out. If she had died, she would have been Denton's twelfth victim, but the only one to have died by gun shot.

Alena had worked on the Denton case for four months before she got a break in the case, a slipup that connected all eleven murders over the course of fifteen years. All the rope used in the torture of his victims was the same brand and thickness, but never the same color. The lab had run the fibers through their databases, but the result wasn't good. Eight unsolved homicides popped with the fibers being a match. The problem wasn't more cases but other jurisdictions, making this a federal case.

Alena did not want to lose this case. She called the officers assigned to the other cases in hopes of garnering more information. Each officer gave her the same information. The details of the bodies are different but definitely staged, it was meant to be seen. The room was otherwise clean, without blood spatter, and with limited forensics to the gruesome scene. The murder weapon was different each time, but every time rope was involved, whether to tie hands or strangulation. One victim even had her hands tied behind her back as she exsanguinated from two slits along the main artery in her wrists. Denton was careful, until now. He had left letters to each victim, giving vivid details to how he would kill them. Finally, they had a Modes Operandi. Eight different cases, eight different states, one MO. The last three cases bookended the other eight, all taking place in LA. His first victim being fifteen years ago, and one five years after that, then his most recent being six months ago. Alena hadn't had a lead until this rope started to thread the clues together.

She needed another break. Detective Martin had an idea, but it was risky. She called and went in to talk to her commanding officer Sargent Richard Essman, who then took her to Captain Ophelia Barton, the real boss.

Alena went in starting with her idea before Captain Barton could even speak. She wanted to have a press conference. Having a press conference could flesh him out and maybe he could slip enough for them to catch him. It was risky, but with little resistance her bosses okayed the idea. The department set it up with Detective Alena Martin as the mouthpiece for the case. Dressed in her formal uniform, Alena addressed the public. She gave limited information, mostly warnings of the letters. Reminding people to let the police know, immediately, if anyone received any suspicious mail or unwarranted attention. They didn't give a description because they truthfully didn't have one, but the one piece they held back was the ropes. She wrapped the conference with a reminder to let the police do their jobs and gave the hotline number setup for any and all tips from the public. She remembered it being short and to the point.

The next day things changed. Alena walked from her apartment to work and had noticed someone following her. The day after that the phone calls came. The single time Alena was there to pick up the phone, the call was not long enough to trace. A week after the press conference the pictures came. Alena came into work a bit earlier than normal. When she walked to her desk, she noticed photographs neatly displayed on top of her files. The letter with her name written in a calligraphic font was gently placed on top. The photographs were of her, her mother, and even a photograph of her at the dinner table by herself. *He had been here.* Frozen she stood, staring at the photographs. Fear slowly gripping as she realized how close he had been, she had never seen his face. Joni, her partner, had to snap her out of it. The forensic team was called after the squad was told to not touch anything and to walk out, the precinct was being treated like a crime scene.

Later that same day, after her desk was cleaned off and made a mess of, Denton called. *Did you get my gift?* The voice on the other line said. She remembered how his voice seemed to grind against the air. Alena had made one impulsive move: she had the Technical Investigating Division keep a tap on her phones on the off chance he got cocky. She had gotten lucky. Alena managed to get him to talk until he asked about the letter, "I hope you read my letter. I so hope you get to her before I do," he had said. She hadn't the chance to grab the letter let alone read it. It was in an evidence bag on the way to the lab for prints. He'd hung up. Leaving that last phrase to penetrate her mind. She immediately got a call following his letting her know they had a trace and location. She could only pray he stayed in that location. Detective Martin called Missing Persons and asked about any missing people in the last two days, one girl of twelve popped.

The force took the threats very seriously, as they should, but it hindered her work on closing the case. She was given a security detail courtesy of LAPD Metro. The only positive about having a security detail was that it extended to her mother. She simply wanted to do her job. She refused to be put out on the sidelines and requested to be there for the arrest.

The LAPD came out in force to the warehouse. They treated the situation as a hostage negotiation with additional federal back up in the form of US Marshalls. Denton refused to talk, he made one demand, to meet Detective Martin. Alena had limited experience with hostage situations, but what she did remember from training was to keep the person talking. She was under qualified, but she was the only one he would talk to. She knew *him,* she knew the details better than anyone. But no one expected the events that ensued. Those events haunted her every sleeping moment.

Alena looked herself in the mirror and stared at herself. She saw a strong woman, her round face with freckles, still young, but the eyes had grown sharp and hard. This wasn't what she thought she'd feel or look like at this stage in life. She needed a break from death. Alena turned the faucet to the hotel shower on hot, she deserved it after all. As she sat and waited for the water to warm, she decided she was going to visit her mother today. She had needed space after the shooting, but two weeks had gone by since she had been shot, it was still all such a blur. She had cut herself away from the world, after the hospital, physical therapy. She had been postponing IAB appointments, psychiatrist appointments, for the past couple of days. Alena Martin was instead staying in a little hotel by the beach. She was only a few miles away if anyone needed her. But her job and life were waiting for her to rejoin it. When she got out of the shower, she changed into a pair of denim skinny jeans, a light V-neck t-shirt, and a pair of heeled booties.

She picked up her phone, 9:30 a.m., her mom would be awake, then she noticed the voicemail symbol on the top of her phone reminders. The Captain had called telling her not to come back until next week, she was putting her on paid leave until next Friday: it was only Wednesday. Alena thought this could be indefinitely until IAB and psych eval came back clean. She understood the protocols, but she did miss the real world.

Before she called her mother, she probably should check in with her partner and check on the caseload that had been dumped onto her plate after Alena was put on leave. She pressed the speed-dial number of her partner, who picked up after her typical three dial tone wait. "Detective Solare, here."

"Hey, Joni."

"Whoa, it's alive," a chuckle came from the phone.

"Yes, I haven't done anything stupider than drink hotel coffee."

"Well, at least you're not as stupid as John was drinking the station coffee."

"When will he learn. But hey I was just calling to check in on that paperwork you got dumped with."

"Ah don't worry about it, just get to feeling better. You have physical therapy appointments to make, IAB to talk to, and the pesky psych evaluation before you are on full duty. You'll be on desk duty for a while, don't worry kiddo, I can almost see my desk. Hey, I heard the Captain has a case for you?"

"What? I haven't heard anything yet."

"You probably won't 'til ya get back."

"Hmm, weird, well, if I hear anything, I let you know." Alena said a bit puzzled and curious.

"Yea, no worries, hey, thanks for the check in kiddo. I was a bit worried about you there."

"I've been calling every day."

"I know, but it just helps to know my partner is safe. Even if I'm benched." Through her husky voice Alena could hear that toothy smile.

Alena chuckled, "Well, the streets are safer without you."

Joni dryly responded "Oh HAR HAR, you should go be a comedienne. Don't quit your day job, call tomorrow, okay?"

"Yea, sure, Joni. Tell Tessa I say hi." Alena hung up the phone and sat on the bed. She saw the time flash on her phone and remembered she was going to call her mother.

She dialed the number, waited three rings, and her mother answered, "Hello, Alena, is that you, sweetheart?"

"Yes, mom, is there any way I can visit, you know for a couple of days, the hotel is beginning to make me feel a bit smothered," Alena asked in a nervous way.

"Of course! When should I expect you?"

"Oh, I can be there in about an hour and a half, or is that too early?" Still groggy she thought about sitting on her mother's couch with a cup of her mother's English tea.

"No, not at all. I will put the tea on when you text me that you are on the way, I will see you soon, I love you sweetheart."

"I love you too Mom."

They both hung up. Alena packed up the stuff she brought with her and checked out over the phone. Once more she caught her reflection in the bathroom mirror and thought she looked nothing like her supposed Greek ancestry, she looked more English, with her northern European blue eyes. She shook her head and walked out. She knew she was adopted but like many adopted children she struggled with the question of why and how she fit in with her small family, she did not look a bit like her adoptive mother and father. She just wished she looked like some member of her family. She sent a brief text stating that she had checked out of the hotel and was walking to the bus stop.

She called IAB. After a brief conversation with the commanding officer setting up an appointment for her come in Friday afternoon. The detective, who met with her first thing after the shooting, was at the hospital. He was nice enough, a bit grey at the temples and made clear that this was not his first or even his hundredth shooting case. The questions were blunt and rote, making it easy to answer them but very hard for Alena to stay awake during

17

the interview, the pain killers saw to that. There was one question that she did remember, it was the only question that wasn't asked in the detective's monotone, *Why and how did he escape?* It was a question she didn't have an answer for.

She called and left a voice mail for the department psychiatrist requesting an appointment. The third bus stop was within walking distance of her mother's house in the Los Angeles suburb of Santa Monica. The walk was slow, her duffle bag kept hitting the side of her right leg, but she was too stubborn to move it to the other side of her body. Her mother was sitting on the stairs of her house, expecting her. Her mother came up to her, eyes level with hers, took the duffle bag off her shoulder and held her in her arms. "I was so scared, Alena, I thought I was going to lose you when I got that phone call" she whispered through her tears. Alena knew which call, the call that Joni had made while in the hospital. Joni had made the phone call that Alexandria had always feared.

"I am so sorry, but I am here, and you will never lose me." A promise she truly couldn't keep in this line of work. Alena moved back to look at her mother, at her beautiful hazel brown eyes. She had always known this beautiful olive-skinned woman, with her beautiful English accented voice as her mother, adopted or biological. She

18

was one of the only people that, when she cried so did Alena. "Tea."

"Sorry?"

"I think I hear the tea pot whistling" Alena clarified, smiling and wiping away her tears.

"Oh!" Her mother grabbed her duffle and hustled Alena into the house and dropped the bag near the front door. Alena knew her way around this house better than her own apartment. She went to the kitchen as her mother was pouring the tea into the pot. Alena took the cream out of the refrigerator before her mother could get to it, placing it next to the sugar and lemons that were already on the table. Her mother smiled, remembering how Alena always helped with tea even as a small child. They sat down together and created their tea and just looked at one another, waiting for the other to start the conversation. Both were still a bit awkward after Alena's father's death a year ago due to a prolonged case of cancer. Her father did see her become a detective, the smile on his face she will never forget. "How are you holding up, after dad—" Alena just let it hang there because she simply did not want to finish the thought. She knew it was going to be a touchy subject, but they had not really talked about it, and with the recent events it was about damn time. Her mother's eyes began to tear up. Her head was in her hands before Alena left her tea and came over to her, grabbed a chair and held her. No words were exchanged for a few moments, until her mother's little terrier, Buddy, nudged both of them. Alena picked up the dog and held him on her lap between the two of them. Scratching the dog's ears was a therapy within itself and comforting for both women. "Well, I am holding up as well as I can, but I don't know how I would have held up if that bullet had hit your heart."

"I know, that is why I am here now, and probably why my captain gave me until Friday. If it is okay with you I will stay with you." Alena requested.

"How's Joni?"

"She's got a ton of paperwork to catch up on from other cases, but otherwise she's good."

Alena took her tea and sat on the couch, on the other side of the house, that had a view of the ocean. Her mother joined her and they chatted, avoiding the two hard topics, Alena's experience and her father's death. They simply caught up, watched a couple of mutual favorite movies, talked about the nice weather, and the recent man in Alena's life, among other things.

"So how is, what is his name, the writer?"

"Nick" Alena stated.

"That's right, how is he?"

"He is good, he has called a few times and I explained that I needed some time, to remember to breathe, but I was going to call him later this week"

"Good, I think you should."

Alena looked at her mother suspicisiously. "I thought you did not like any of the guys I dated after I demanded no matchmaking" Alena smiled.

"I know but this one is different, he respects you and your space."

"He's okay, but I think I want something different than he does, we are really just friends with an attempt to connect. I don't really like him like that." Alena felt the phone vibrate in her back pocket.

"Okay, whatever you say." Her mom smiled a knowingly, "Oh speak of the devil."

Alena rolled her eyes as she answered the call.

Chapter II

Mother and daughter spent the day as though Alena was a child on a school break again. Around 10 pm, Alena received a phone call from her Captain telling her she had a case that she might be interested in and no one else wanted to take, it was a cold case but maybe she could find some new detail.

"I will come in tomorrow and grab the file, if you would like, but yes I accept."

"No, it can wait enjoy your time off. Go see your father. Those files will be there when you get back."

With a sigh "Okay, Cap, see you Friday."

"See you then" and her line clicked, ending the call.

"Mum," the years she spent growing up in England became evident when she was around her mother, "I am going to go ahead and get some sleep" she said aloud as she placed her cell phone into her pocket. She was still standing in the living room with one of the numerous cups of tea she had drank during the day, when her mother came back into the room. The room had changed very little since she had moved to her apartment when she was nineteen. Still hung on the beige walls were a few of the paintings that Alena had painted a few years ago, the purple and gold window curtains still separated to allow natural light in. The furniture was typical but minimal; couch at a ninety-degree angle from and behind the window, the forty-inch flat screen television, typically used for movies or futball matches, on the wall, and the side table with a lamp on the right of the couch. There was also a round rug on top of the bamboo floor but beneath the coffee table. Some would say sparse, Alena said it was neat, but it was always home.

She heard her mother's heeled boots click on the tile of the kitchen and the wooden bamboo in the hallway leading to the living room. "Your room is all set, Ally"

"Thanks, I think I will get some sleep if that is okay? See you in the morning, love you" As she hugged her mother.

"Yes, get some sleep, I love you too, we will talk some more later."

Alena walked down the hallway to the room she had not slept in for nearly ten years, her bag had been placed at the foot of the bed. She changed, got under the covers and fell asleep quickly.

The gun was pointed at her chest, her team was just outside the door, but Denton was not going to talk to anyone except her. She had walked in to the room, a girl of no older than twelve was behind him, the girl he had taken to get the police's attention that he was back in town. Alena did not say anything just pointed her gun at Denton, with her armored vest on her chest. Denton screamed at her to put gun down or the girl dies. Alena lifted her hands after hesitating, making a show of it, she clicked the safety, and placed her gun on the ground. She nudged it a few feet away with her foot. Her eyes never left his; if she was going to get shot, she wanted to see it coming. Alena kept her hands raised. She knew the gun was loaded, but he hadn't pulled the hammer back. Her motions were slow and calculated as she moved back to her standing position. "Hand over the girl" stated Alena. Denton gestured that it was okay for the girl to leave. She ran to Alena, who backed up to the door with the girl behind her. Denton gestured with his gun that Alena was not allowed to leave by cocking the gun. Alena moved back and asked what he wanted, they already had his confession, evidence, plenty for a clean conviction. Alena stood and listened to for every gruesome detail about how he was planning to torture, rape and then kill her. He was going to send a piece of her to her mother. That was new. He was changing. That was when Alena moved for her second gun behind her left hip, before she had her hand on it, she heard the gun shot.

Alena woke up with a start. She had relived this memory over and over again for the past several weeks in her sleep. Since she was already wide awake, she gave up going back to sleep. She turned on her light and changed to go to a walk along the sandy beach not far from the house. Her mother was drowsily standing in her doorway before she grabbed her shoes. Alena had forgotten how light a sleeper her mother was "Was your nightmare that bad?"

Alena nodded her head, "if you want, I will tell you..." it was then as she stood up that her shirt was lifted just long enough for her mother to see the damage of the gun shot.

Her mother shook her head "Just give me a second."

They were both in sweats and t-shirts and they put on closed-toe slip-ons as they walked out the door, Buddy sleepily whimpering in his dog bed. It was still was small hours when they walked out and breathed in the chilled air. They walked along the sand a while before Alena's mother asked about the scar almost apologetically "Does it still hurt?"

"When I stretch and run"

"So, what happened…at the warehouse?"

"Do you really want to know?"

They stopped and sat on a couple of smoother rocks on the beach. Alena kicked off her shoes and started digging her toes into the cold dry sand. Alena explained as much as she could, leaving out some details including how her body would have been delivered to her mother in pieces and what would have happened to her if she had been kidnapped by this creep.

They sat in silence for a while; just listening to the waves hit the sand. Alena looked to her mother's regal and noble face in profile, as the tears of pain stung her eyes. Alena let the tears fall freely, they were the first real tears that she had had since before her dad passed away. In fact, she really did not even cry at her father's funeral, she had to be strong for her mother and family, she was not allowed to break. Every pain she had ever faced, every face she saw in a homicide case file, and every moment she wanted to walk away, every pain from this last case, her father's death: everything came rushing forward.

Alexandria looked at her daughter and understood the pain she was finally releasing and simply held her daughter. At length, after allowing the tears to fall Alexandria said, "Let's go make some coffee and breakfast okay?" In response, Alena stood tall, wiped away the tears on her face and walked back to the house with her mother.

Chapter III

Time moved slowly the following day, though it was nice for once to sleep, to talk, and not have anything to do but snuggle with Buddy. It was nice to be around the last piece of family she had.

Her mother was a retired archaeologist that got out of the field a few years ago when Alena's father first got sick, and never went back to academia. Even though she was retired, Dr, Alexandria Martin, by no means slacked in anything. She would put her whole heart into it something, some called her ambitious, but it was one of Alena's favorite qualities about her mother. For as long as Alena could remember her mother had strong features; prominent straight nose, hazel eyes, dark brown long hair and olive skin with a curvy frame of five foot three, though no one would know as she always wore heels. She was always so regal and noble in anything she did or anything she wore, even when she was in sweats. She always looked different than Alena, with her blue eyes, round face, fair skin, and red-brown hair, which just helped to confirm the fact of her being adopted. Her father was a strong-featured man, green eyes, dark blond hair about six feet tall. He was an ambassador for antiquities. They met at a conference for international law, they were both guest speakers. Both were up and coming big shots in their fields of study and careers and has to deal with finding a balance, but they married two years later.

Alena was born and adopted by her parents two years later and grew up in England for about thirteen years, before the family decided to move back to her father's hometown of Los Angeles, California. Alena was academically ahead of her class and graduated early from high school at sixteen and did not really know what she wanted to do as a career. It was her father who suggested she go into criminology, after seeing her love of mysteries and eye for even the smallest of details. She later graduated from college early as well with honors and attended the Los Angeles police academy. She even put in an application with the FBI, but they wanted her to have more experience. Alena enjoyed searching for details and viewing the cases as mysteries to be solved instead of homicide cases to be closed, which allowed her to look at every case individually instead of them blending together.

Alena was sitting at the table thinking about the past few years and wondering about the next few, simply thinking, avoiding any thought involving work tomorrow. She did not even realize her mother had placed a plate in front of her until the third time she called her name, "Hmm? I am sorry what were you saying?" she said a bit dazed.

"Are you okay?"

"Yeah, I'm fine...why?"

"Well, for one you haven't even touched your breakfast, I made your favorite apples and cinnamon sweet potato pancakes and some turkey bacon. I even made your favorite coffee." she laughed lightly, "Are you really okay, Ally?"

Alena looked at the plate in front of her, and finally the sweet cinnamon reached her nose, "I will be, just give me some time, and hugs, I have to heal on my own" as she reached and gripped her mother's hand for the comfort, she rarely allowed herself. She spread some butter on the two medium sized pancakes and just picked them up and ate them as if they were pieces of toast.

"I am glad that hasn't changed" Alexandria said as she shook her head and smiled.

They enjoyed their time for breakfast and sipped their coffee sitting on the couch and watching the waves. Alena rarely had time for things like watching waves, or ~~just~~ enjoying her coffee instead of gulping it to stay awake. It was therapeutic in a way to be away from work and most distractions. She remembered to call Nick, but his phone was off, so she just left a message asking him to call her back when he could. For most of her time off she just spent it reading, walking along the beach, and simply relaxing something she could not remember doing since she was a young girl in London. She finally did get really curious about that cold case and decided to call her Captain and ask a few questions.

"Good morning, Captain."

"Morning, Martin, what can I do for you, on your day off?" said the familiar female voice of her captain.

"I was just curious about this cold case, how long has it been inactive? And why me?"

"Don't worry about it, we'll have a long conversation about it when you get back in two days, take a break and read a book and go see your mom, okay, and tell her I said hi?"

"Okay, but Captain I—"

"I know, but that's an order, enjoy your time, heal, I will see you tomorrow." Her captain then hung up, leaving Alena a bit confused. She had never really had a cold case and her captain would usually indulge her questions. Her captain knew that she liked a bit of a feel for the case even before she got into the file. Alena turned around and was startled to see her mother, as though she was getting ready to reach out. After catching their breath, Alexandria explained, "I did not mean to scare you, but it seems we scared each other" she smiled, "Was that your Captain?"

"Yeah, but she didn't answer any of my questions, she really kind of evaded them," she sighed heavily and ran her fingers through her hair and said almost to herself. "It was strange."

"What is this about a cold case?" after seeing the look on her daughter's face, "You know I never got out of the business, I am too curious not to overhear."

"You mean eavesdrop."

"Fine, but maybe I could help."

"But that's just it, I don't know anything, but I will concede it would be interesting working with you, but you know I can't."

"Not without proper clearance." Alexandria smiled mischievously.

"I will talk and see what I can figure out from my Captain, but I still just want to relax and remember how to breathe before I go back."

"I understand, but can I see your scar? Or is that too much…"

"No" Alena said as she simply lifted the cotton shirt, she was wearing just enough to see the bullet wound.

The entry wound was just a bit bigger than her pinky finger and the exit wound on the other side was about the size of her thumb. The scar tissue had already healed for the most part but was still a bit tender as her mother traced the hole with her finger gently, "I am so sorry, sweetheart" as she lifted her eyes to her daughters.

"Armor piercing. Causes more damage. Hurt like nothing I have ever felt before, but I lived."

***

Alena fell asleep that night on the couch watching TV. She was on her side still dressed in her day clothes. Buddy, the little terrier, was curled up next to Alena's abdomen asleep. Alexandria still heard the TV on at around one in the morning and decided to check on her daughter. As she suspected she fell asleep while watching a crime show. She put the pillow Alena had made in a sewing class, underneath her head and a blanket that Alexandria knitted years ago over her. Alena's phone buzzed with a text. Alexandria only flipped it long enough to see the sender's name: Nick. She placed the phone back down on the table. She brushed her daughter's hair out of her face, then scratched the dog's ears and went back to her bedroom. Not fifteen minutes passed when she heard her daughter start. Alexandria walked back swiftly still not wanting to wake Alena, until she heard her scream "No!"

Alexandria shook Alena to wake her from the repetitive nightmare. She looked wide-eyed and panicked as though she did not recognize anything that surrounded her. Buddy jumped off the couch and moved to the arm chair and fell back asleep. Alena was breathing heavily and sweating, she began to cry as Alexandria held her in her arms as she had many times before, and often in the past few days. Alena fell asleep in her mother's arms. Alexandria placed her daughter's head back onto the pillow Alena made and replaced the blanket. Alexandria fell asleep in the armchair watching her daughter sleep, knowing there was something Alena had not told her.

The next morning Alexandria let her daughter sleep, after turning Alena's alarm off. She decided to make breakfast and coffee around ten in the morning. Alena was awake when she heard the coffee grinder start and smelled the faint scent of toasted bread. Alena sat there for a few minutes on the couch as she rubbed the sleep out of her eyes, stretched, and then cringed. Her scar stretched as she did but still was tight and tender as she moved. She moved to sit with her feet on the ground and rubbed her toes, through her socks, on the bamboo floor. She was in the lounge shorts and long cotton t-shirt she wore yesterday. She stood and walked into the kitchen, where the smell of black coffee was strong and sat at the table. Without a word, her mother placed a plate with a sliced, toasted bagel in front of her. Then she placed the Greek yogurt cream cheese in the middle between them. Alena got up and got a cup of coffee, with a bit of cream, and sat and sipped.

"Did you sleep well?" Alexandria asked, curious if her daughter remembered the nightmare.

"I was restless." She shrugged it off, not really wanting to talk about it.

"What was the nightmare about? Do you remember waking up last night?"

She stopped mid bite, finished the bite and chewed slowly.

"Alright, I get it. You will talk about it when you want to..." as she shrugged and sipped her coffee. Alexandria was still in her pajamas and robe, but more out of comfort versus being tired. She was worried, like any mother, but wanted to give her space as well as her own time to heal. Still, she wanted to help and find out what all happened. Tomorrow was the day that Alena was to go back to work and her own place, so long as she felt up to it. Alena had talked about moving back in but still wanted to be on her own, as if she had something to prove, she was always a stubborn child. She had lived on her own since she was nineteen; when she left for college to live in the dorms. Then, in her junior year moved in with a good friend until she found a place available in the same apartment complex. Since her father died, she had thrown herself into her work and was not in her apartment much.

"Look, sweetheart, we need to talk" Alexandria stated in her English accent, gently yet as authoritative as felt necessary. Alena's phone rang, she flipped it over, and swiped it to silent mode.

"Mum, I will but—" as she bit into her bagel her mother interrupted.

"No, last night was the line. I need to know what happened."

"What are you talking about?" Alena asked genuinely confused.

"You don't remember waking up last night, do you?"

"No."

"You were terrified, that is understandable, but I need to know so I can help"

"Maybe you should have been a shrink instead of an archaeologist" she smiled sadly as she knew that this conversation was going to come up, she had just hoped later.

"It had crossed my mind" as Alexandria shrugged.

Alena breathed in deeply as she bought herself a bit of time to remember everything she left out. She exhaled as she began to explain what she had left out, this time she didn't even leave out what would have happened if she had been kidnapped. Her mother stayed quiet throughout, but was shocked, and her eyes widened as she heard the details of what would have been her daughter's torture and later death. There was a long pause as Alena checked the time on her phone and realized the date, that today her supposed vacation time was over as her shift was going to begin in two hours at around one pm.

"Shit!" she said almost as if under her breath.

"What?" Alexandria asked after sipping coffee.

"I can go back, I have to get ready and at least look like I got some sleep" she jokingly smiled as she stood up and headed to the shower. It took her just ten minutes to take her shower; she then changed into a pair of dark denim jeans, and a light blouse in blue and then zipped her grey

37

booties onto her feet. She tussled her hair and put on her face, and then was out the door with her keys and gun in her shoulder holster under her neutral leather jacket in five minutes after saying she would be back soon.

Chapter IV

"Have you talked to IAB, yet?"

This was the first question the Captain asked when Alena got back to the precinct. Not even really a simple hello. Alena took public transportation to get to the station as she did not feel like going back to her apartment to get her car. She listened softly to her iPod on her way to LAPD Headquarters, downtown partly to ignore people and yet still soft enough that she was well aware of her surroundings. Her badge was on her belt, easily viewable. She got off and walked the few blocks from the stop to the precinct at a comfortable pace even though she was late, wanting to enjoy the last moments on her morning. She took her head phones out once she was only one block from the precinct.

She walked into the building and walked up the stairs to the floor for homicide and opened the door. She walked passed her desk and straight to the Captain as she had many questions she wanted answered. However, it was the Captain that really threw her off as she opened the Captain's office door. Even as Alena turned around, she was already partially spoken into a question that Alena did not expect.

"Have you seen IAB,yet?"

"Yes," Alena hesitated to state, quizzically after a short pause, "I was going to see them this afternoon."

"Good, because you are going to desk duty until they clear you."

"What? Captain, you might as well keep my gun. I am fine, really."

Frustrated, Alena sighed and just looked at her Captain. Her Captain was one of the few female captains; she was a beautiful woman with brown eyes and brown hair, in her early forties but did not look it. She was a very focused woman and determined in her job, similar to Alena, which is a reason why she was both hard on her force and yet very understanding. She knew how to give her squad space, like this last case. Right now, she knew Alena's reaction all too well, as she had expressed it often enough to her own Captain, when she just wanted to focus on her work and not herself. She looked the young detective in the eyes and realized for the umpteenth time how young she really was.

"I understand that, but I am giving you a new assignment. Plus, until IAB and the psych eval clears you, you're benched, and don't worry about your service weapon." She tapped her desk making a point that it was safe.

Confused Alena said, "But you just said you were just giving me a case."

"I am. I am giving you something to work on, something that you might be interested in."

"Oh?"

"A cold case, I received a phone call from a business man, wanting a cold case opened."

"A cold case, how cold of a case?" Alena asked still really confused.

"Thirty-five years, but it is unique and unsolved, he wants it to be looked at again, and asked for the best, so I gave it to you." Her captain closed the file after she placed a piece of paper into it. She handed the thick file to Alena, "Here… Further instructions are on the piece of paper, and you can always call if you need more information. Oh! and don't forget to check in with me and the shrink next week."

"Captain, what am I going to see that someone in the past thirty-five years has not, and am I allowed to bring anyone into the case for assistance or specific perspectives?" Ignoring the hint about seeing the precinct shrink. She hated talking to psychiatrist, she'd rather have a cup of tea and talk to her mum than talk to someone she didn't really know.

"You sound as though you have someone in mind…"

"Not yet," But Alena had been thinking of someone, but wanted to get her input before asking for her skills in areas Alena was not very familiar with that may help with certain things.

"If you want, ask Joni, she's had a case or two go cold, she might help you with that perspective, she's your partner for a reason."

"Understood, I am curious, before I really accept this, is there anything specific that is not in the file?"

"You might want to talk to Interpol and get their information on this case or make a phone call to the two numbers on the paper."

"Interpol, ah shit, Captain that is not going to get far."

"That's why I gave you the numbers," her Captain smiled, as she knew that Alena would be the best for this, because she was willing to bend the rules, instead of breaking them. She was focused and determined and always saw things differently as well as being able to maneuver around obstacles well.

Alena walked out the office with the file in hand and open, but not without shaking her head first and muttering something about the case being simply something to do. Alena grabbed a cup of coffee and sat at her desk, which for the first time in months, was clear of paperwork.

Joni walked up to their shared desk setup and sat down, the stack of paperwork had shrunk since Alena left but was still enough to keep Joni busy. "Hey kiddo," Said Joni, "New business I take it, what is it?"

"Cold case," She sipped the coffee, and then pushed it away thinking she'd get a cup later from elsewhere. Their shared desk had a bit of clutter with files and the small personal items. Joni had the Denton case file on her side of the desk. As she flipped it open, Alena had a glimpse of the picture of the man. His cold dark eyes were like staring into the deepest chasms of the earth. Hair the color of dirt with creamy white skin. His face a juxtaposition of clean and dirty. When he spoke, he had a voice roughened by years of packs of cigarettes a day. He was a juxtaposition of clean and dirty, almost like a demented toy maker pieced him together with leftovers. Alena was snapped out of it when she realized Joni asked for a pen. Without a word Alena handed her a blue ink pen. Joni had a couple photo frames with a picture of her schnauzer and her wife Tessa to the side of her computer monitor. Alena had a selfie photo of her mom and her with, Buddy tapped to the corner of her monitor, and a glass paperweight holding a never-ending pile of files.

Joni stood up to throw her jacket on and offered the pen back.

"No, keep it. I've several of them,"

"Nice---" Joni was interrupted by the phone ringing.

"Detective Solare, here."

Alena looked up and felt the urge to ask what was happening and whisper, "who is it?"

"Tessa, has to take the dog to the vet and can't find the files. But I got a text from the lab for a copy of a report I need for my files."

"Tell Tessa, hi, what's wrong with Scruffs" the schnauzer's name was Mr. Scruffy.

"Oh, it's just his annual appointment"

"Gotcha, no worries, let Cap know,"

Joni nodded, as she continued to listen to Tessa talk about the information that she misplaced.

but remembered she was put at her desk with this new case. She waited until Joni hung up. Joni Solare was easily fifteen years older than Alena with shoulder-length brunette hair she almost always kept out of her face and clear green eyes. She had a great laugh and sense of humor, but always called Alena "kiddo". Which was fine if Joni did it, but annoying when anyone else did. Joni wasn't thin, but fit and strong and almost always managed to get Alena to the mat when they sparred against each other. Alena knew her partner had her back, no matter what. Joni grabbed her badge and gun that were on the desk before she hung up.

"Got to go kiddo, I'll help you out with that case if you want, you've got my number" she said as she quickly headed for the door.

Joni was long gone, and Alena was reading the file before she heard the door open to the department and then close again. Several times she heard the department office doors open and close as many of the officers came and went. Many greetings from her colleagues as they passed to desks or file cabinets. Sargent Rick walked up with a cup of coffee in hand, "Hey, Martin, how are you doing?"

"I'm as good as can be expected,"

"What do you have there?"

45

"Just a cold case, I am just familiarizing myself with the details, before going to sources."

"Sounds good, let me know if you need anything, even if it's just a coffee."

"I was going to get something other than that mud," Alena laughed at the idea, "But thanks, Sargent, I appreciate it and I'll keep in mind."

He nodded with a knowing smile and walked towards the other side of the room. Alena reached for the bottom right draw of her desk for her water bottle that she always kept at work when she felt a hand on her back. She wasn't startled because she had heard the voice that went with it, moments earlier. She knew exactly who it was. Her best friend from university stood behind her. They both had decided to go into criminology, but she had gone into writing novels in the end and Alena added the double major for forensic archaeology. Since Alena had been able to test out of large parts of the archaeology major it only added a few classes to what remained in her degree and they graduated together. Stevie was easily 5 feet 5 inches, with warm blue-green eyes and long medium brown hair that would look almost blonde on the brightest of summer days. She had a rather young face, but she was roughly eight years older than Alena. When they were at university, Stevie was there for her Master's degree after taking some time off while Alena was a first time student. She was a little heavier set than Alena but not by much and she carried herself well.

"Hey, Alena, how are you doing?"

"Hmm…" Alena was very distracted as she had started to really become interested in the cold case file.

"How are you?" she asked again patiently.

"Oh, sorry Stevie" she went for the cup of coffee but remembered when she got it and looked at her watch and decided against taking a sip. "In all honesty, I am a bit of a mess, but I will manage, like always."

"Sometimes I worry that you are too stubborn and will work until you really crash."

"Don't. I know I will be fine, I just need time, Stevie."

"You seem really involved, why don't we go grab a bite to eat, our favorite sushi place is open, I'll buy this time."

"Alright, but I am taking the file." She gave her friend a look of finality and grabbed her jacket—open file in hand, messenger bag over her shoulder.

***

TEA TIME

They were just being served when Stevie asked, "What is this one all about, a murder, kidnapping oh or is it a medical malpractice?"

"Stevie, you are mental," without looking up from the file.

"I know. That's why my name is on a bunch of crime novels: Stephanie Wesgaur." She said it as though it would impress anyone, but Alena knew she was just kidding around. Stevie smiled and looked at her best friend for further details. Alena smiled and shook her head but still didn't look from the file, she even tried to eat part of her sushi roll with chopsticks. Stevie put her hand in Alena's line of vision and closed the file "Eat."

There was no arguing. Though they were best friends they acted more like very close sisters, and Alena knew that Stevie was just looking out for her. She put the file aside and enjoyed her sushi. Until, "So, which is it?" Stevie asked, almost as though the question was asked every day, and in her case in a way, it was.

Alena rolled her eyes and put another piece of sushi in her mouth to avoid the question. She chewed the question in her head as she chewed her food, sushi swallowed, she knew she was going to have to answer because Stevie would just pose it again later if she did not. Knowing full well the answer before she even posed the question, she still figured it would be good to ask it, if for nothing more than good measure, "Can you keep secrets?"

The look on her friend's face was almost as though Alena had insulted her, but she still answered, "Yes, what is this about?"

"The case, it's a cold case about thirty-five years old."

"I am confused, why would your Captain give you something like that?"

"To figuratively keep me at my desk, but I was thinking, I could use your thoughts on this case.," After seeing the puzzling look on Stevie's face "My Captain wants to keep me from cases where I could get hurt again and with me still recouping, she wanted to keep me busy but not really. She gave me leave until deemed fully healed and cleared." Alena said the last part sarcastically as she did not like taking required help, ever. This was only her second shooting, but it wasn't a very clean shoot, lots of questions and issues that IAB got involved. She still wasn't one to complain about her issues, she signed up for it, so she'll deal with it. She knew better than anyone when she needed it, and when to ask, and when she did not want it at all.

TEA TIME

The check came and before Alena could even fight for it, Stevie tucked her card into the sleeve and slid it to the end of the table.

"I told you it was my turn" she smiled.

"It's always your turn, I never can get the check before you do."

Stevie just shrugged and smiled, signed the slip when it came back and waited for Alena to put the cold case file in her messenger bag. Alena decided to check her watch for the time. She knew it was time to go home, as she was not needed at the precinct. Stevie caught an Uber, while Alena parted to walk home.

"You sure I cant give you a ride?"

"No, I am good, I'm headed to my mum's, shes only a couple blocks for here. It's good for me to smell the roses every now and again."

Stevie nodded and closed the door, just as Alena's phone rang, it was Nick.

"Hello?" Alena answered but wasn't sure where this conversation would go.

"It's Nick, I was just checking on you with everything, I kinda figured you wanted some space but I also wanted to see if you were up for a third date?"

"Oh right, no, I'm good, what do you mean by everything?"

50

"Didn't you say you were doing something for your parents this week, I just didn't want to impose."

"Yeah, right, um sure I can check my schedule and get back to you for sure. So how's the news?"

"Oh, it always needs to be written."

"Great, Hey can I call you back I have another call coming in."

"Yea, of course."

The other caller was Joni.

"Hey, how's Scruffy?"

"He's healthy as ever, I was just checking on you, let me know if you need any help with that cold case, it could be a good one."

"I will thanks, give Scruffy ear scratches from me."

"Of course,"

"I'll text you when I'm home."

"Good, catch you soon," Alena hung up the phone. She walked another block and saw the warm blossoms and blooms in her mother's small front of house garden. The roses were not yet in full bloom, but the fragrant smell of petals filled her nose. Spring was definitely here. The pollen was in the air and Alena was already paying for it with her sinuses. She at least remembered to take an antihistamine today, keeping the pollen at bay, allowing her to enjoy the soft smell of the flowers in the trees along the path home. Some of her mother's neighbors had trees in full bloom and the sweet fragrance had the miraculous ability to cut through the smell of the city. Alena walked to the door, as she still had not braved going to her apartment to get her car even yet. She put the spare key into the door and opened it, breathing it the smell of spring before walking in.

Her mother was watching a futbol match on the television as Alena sat on the couch pulling out the file to yet again get lost in the clues and hunt for the answers. She was interrupted by the occasional swear word from her mother as an enthusiastic fan. She eventually realized her mother had turned on the light, the game was over and won, by the English team, her team, and she was hungry. She rubbed her eyes as she heated leftovers for herself and poured a glass of water. Her mother came in and went to the fridge for the same reason as Alena. They sat together at the table Alena had gone back to grab the file as her food was heating. The tupperware container was on the table with a fork in it when she came back. She started to read the file and again began to block everything out, until, for the second time today there was a hand in her line of vision, between her and the file.

"Take a break and talk to your mother…" it was not a request. Alexandria grabbed the file and closed it, setting it aside so as to look at her daughter and have a conversation. It had not been too long since Alena had engrossed herself in a case, the last time Alexandria had almost lost her.

"So, what do you want to talk about?" Alena asked nonchalantly.

"Well, for starters, how was your day? And then why are you so taken with this cold case?" Without asking Alena knew that her mother had looked at the file, looking over her shoulder thinking she wouldn't notice. "Well, my day was okay, I had a meeting with the Captain who gave me this case and promptly relieved me to my own devices. I then had lunch with Stevie and came home. But I do not really know why this cold case, I don't even know why I was assigned this case outside of being desked." Alena sighed and shrugged. She ate some more of the pasta leftovers and was just thinking when she realized what today was: her father's birthday, April 29. That explained why her mother was watching a match played by his favorite team, Manchester United. She reached across the table and held her mother's hand. "We can go tomorrow, I forgot, I am sorry."

"I know, it's okay."

"I know that you have footy games recorded that you haven't watched yet." She smiled as she began to pick up the containers. "Maybe this time I will understand the rules of the game" Alena laughed.

"I will go and get it set up" Alexandria smiled.

They went to sleep shortly after the second recorded match, and again another nightmare. Alena needed to breath. She walked to the balcony window to feel the air.

The house was two leveled. The kitchen and the living space were on the bottom floor while the bedrooms and balcony were on the second floor. A short wide hallway resided between the balcony and the stairs. In a small space beyond the bedroom doors, her mother had created an alcove, she called it her mini library. She sat in one of the chairs feeling the night air breathe through the window, crisp and clean. It was the crisp air before summer that would warm in the daylight but send shivers down the spine once the stars showed. She stared at those waves for several minutes before she was ready to go back in and try to sleep.

***

She awoke early the next morning, with a surprising feel of rested relief. Maybe she was going to get over these nightmares. She got dresses and for a pleasant change made her mother breakfast. She found a couple apples and pears in the refrigerator as well as some strawberries. Alena cleaned them off, sliced and diced them and mixed them in a bowl. She then grabbed the large container of Greek yoghurt out of the refrigerator and separated some into two small bowls. She looked for some of the clover honey her mother always kept in the cabinet and placed in next to the bowls. She then remembered the granola her mother made earlier in the week and hoped there was some left. Gratefully there was. She scooped a spoonful onto each bowl of yoghurt and the put some of the mixed fruit and lightly drizzled the honey on top. Just as she placed them on the table and turned to make coffee, her mother walked into the kitchen doorway. "Well, how thoughtful."

"I figured something light, this morning wouldn't be such a bad idea."

They sat as the coffee finished, the table was already set, and they ate their breakfast quietly. The two women put their dishes into the dishwasher, and finished their morning routine; fed the dog, got changed and showered, and put up the baby gate in the kitchen for Buddy. After locking the door, they walked to cemetery a few blocks away, where the marker of a beloved father lay.

It was still early but only just, when they walked onto the pavement that wove through the grassy plots. Countless headstones and stone-mason crafted statues littered the green earth. So dark the feeling of death that wafted in the air with a strange contrast to the beautiful morning. Peaceful, strangely peaceful, as though nothing on earth had ever changed but the number of markers. The trees glowed with a faint mist that spread to the dew on the grass between stone. It was so quiet that if one listened closely the whispers of the blades to the leaves could be heard.

The cemetery had only just unlocked their wrought iron gate minutes before. As they closed in the corner that was before the entrance to the patch of green that was Alena's father final resting place. He had always liked the trees that had been planted here. Her mother held their traditional bouquet of flowers that she deposited every other week. A different type of flower every time. This week were a combination of bright blue forget-me-nots and a bundle of light lavender gladiolus both from the garden. She placed them in the small holder that wasn't quite flushed with the ground level.

"Do you remember the significance of the flowers?" she asked as she reached for Alena's hand.

"I know their meaning," Alena knew the meaning and the significance but also knew that her mother needed to say it out loud.

"The forget-me-not was the first flower your father gave to me, the first time we departed from each other, and every time after. The gladiolus was his favorite flower, he always loved the scent, he said it reminded him of me."

Her mother barely held back the tears, it had only been a year, and this was the first of his birthdays to pass without him. Alena knew that the only reason her mother had celebrated any other holiday was for her benefit, if it had been just her mother—Alena didn't want to think of such a lonely idea. She just held her mother's hand and stared at the letters of her father's name in stone.

The gray granite had flecks of iridescent stone sprinkled throughout giving it an eerily beautiful quality. The name was cleaning etched then painted white, to clearly contrast from the stone and color, void of any life just like the body dressed in his suit six feet below the cold hard earth. So very permanent, sharp, and defeating were those letters but she stared at them and remembered them even as her eyes closed.

Michael Martin
beloved father, husband
who served for peace in this world

TEA TIME

No matter how many times or for how long she stared, the etched letters never disappeared, and her father's voice was never heard again.

Chapter V

Sita Richards was a student assistant to Dr. Jansen on the dig in Alexandria, Egypt. She was trying to finish her credits early so she could travel before the perspective as an archaeologist changed the magic she saw into explainable science. She had worked with Dr. Jansen on a dig two years ago and had asked if she could assist with anything on this one. She was fascinated by the history of Egypt and had to basically beg her current professor to give her university credit for this dig as interim experience.

Her long dark hair was pulled back, exposing her rich caramel skin to the elements Sita's black framed Ray-Ban glass had to be pushed up every few minutes due to the size of Dr. Jansen's tiny writing. She was one of the many ethnically diverse members of this truly international crew of anthropologists, forensic and archaeological alike in a wide group of fields. They even had an experimental engineer on the team. She felt so honored to be a part of such a special dig. This was one of those rare sites that might uncover a building like a temple or tombs. With all of the pottery and scroll fragments she's been cataloging, that's how it looked. It was such a rare type of dig that made her parents proud. She remembered their faces when she told them all of the details, she thought they might even be prouder than her brother the lawyer, even for only a moment.

She had always tried to please her parents. She was still single, which was a sore point with her Indian mother, but she didn't want the responsibility of a marriage and children right now. Her Guyanese father told her not to worry, that she would find someone in a town of millions. He meant the city she called home—New York. She was working on her master's degree and worked part-time as a tour guide of the Natural History Museum.

Site Richards loved working there. There was nothing more that she loved that learning, except maybe sharing her knowledge with others. She loved to read and learn about anything and everything. Sita Richards was known for always having a book with her, not an electronic book but a real book, no matter what. One of her favorite things in the whole world was the smell of wisdom between the dry pages of a book. She was very smart but always open for a discussion of ideas and even the occasional friendly debate. She truly believed that she would learn something new every day until her last breath. Her father always said she had "the soul of a scholar", it was one of the reasons she reached for anthropology and now archaeology, was this insatiable drive to learn the answer to why humans are the way they are. It was the ultimate quest for Sita.

She was organizing the pieces of pottery from the day's dig when she heard the tent flap open. She had not realized how late it was getting, the golden grains of sand had settled, the sky was blending into a pale orange. She could smell the salt in the air wafting from the Mediterranean Sea. It was so strong that she could feel the beach between her toes and the water burying her skin into the foam. The sounds of the inner city blurred into a hum on the southern outskirts of ancient city. Sita closed her eyes and breathed in Alexandria deeply, it was such a different feeling than smelling New York. It was cleaner, older somehow.

Sita thought about the method for keeping the order of the dig site specimens. She was always reminding herself so as to never forget: handle the specimen with care, if gloves are available, *use them*, **always**, if not try to handle the specimen through the baggie, examine specimen, identify the specimen, write in down, categorize based on observation, use that number for the label, give it another number for the tag, write everything down on the master copy, *NEVER* lose master copy. These steps she repeated to herself often enough that it had become a mantra.

Taking a breath, she gently hunched back over her labels and tags and opened her eyes. Sita saw a pair of sneakers that hadn't been there before. She looked up when she finished writing the last letter of her catalog description on the master copy then on the label attached to the specimen container.

"Oh! Hi, Peter, what can I do for you?"

"I was just wondering what we picked up today."

Sita was not the biggest fan of Peter. They had met six months earlier, while she was still at Oxford for her semester abroad. She was auditing a sophomore undergraduate level anthropology class, but she wanted a review before plunging into the rest of the course load. Peter was taking the class as a full-time student, or so she thought, but he felt a little old to be in a sophomore course and have no interest in the subject. Typically, the students she met, regardless of age had a bit of enthusiasm for the subject. It wasn't a major you could complete with half the work. He felt too new to anthropology and archaeology to be on a dig, but it was not up to her who she worked with in some cases. Granted, Sita had only been on four other digs but she at least knew what she was doing. There was just something odd about him that she didn't like. But she stayed civil with him, despite her feelings.

"Well, it's a bunch of Hellenistic pottery fragments, and scroll fragments nothing really epic yet." Sita was really excited about what they were hoping to find on this dig, but she didn't want to get her hopes to high, she knew they may not find the tomb or temples until the next dig season.

"Sita, I was wondering if you wanted to get a bite to eat, I noticed you hadn't had dinner." Peter said a little clumsily. Sita knew he was a good-looking guy by anyone's standard, but she couldn't fathom why he was so awkward around women.

"Umm, sure, where was that falafel stand or that little local restaurant that we went to as a group a couple days ago?"

"Yea, that sounds good. Are you good to go now or do you need some help with cleaning up?"

"Nah, I am good," Sita's ponytail fell over her shoulders as she leaned down to put everything in its place, carefully before she once again pushed up her glasses and left. She zipped the tent up and walked a few paces behind Peter until she caught up.

TEA TIME

The next morning Sita Richards did not show up at the fragments station tent, nor she did not answer her phone. Only a note for Dr. Jansen handed to her by Sita's roommate.

Chapter VI

Mother and daughter headed back home. Though nothing productive was done the sadness had drained much of the energy between the two women. Alexandria stopped at the mail box, while Alena let herself into the house, sat on the couch and closed her eyes. Only for a moment were her eyes closed when her mother came rushing in. "Mom, what is it?"

"I got a letter for a friend who needs my help on a dig site," she hurriedly read the letter in her hand and then saw the postage and date on the envelope, "She's in Egypt! But her dig, when she told me, was in Greece what is she doing in Egypt?"

"Well, read the letter and find out," Alena remarked as she looked for the file for the cold case, wanting to pick up where she had left off. Alexandria reread the letter aloud:

I am excited to tell you that this journey has been more enlightening than I expected. More connections

between our work has been discovered and I need your
eyes to see the words of the pages once lost to time. If your
daughter is available, her perspective would be greatly
appreciated. I will send you an email with more
information and details but only trust me. These obstacles
have even me concerned. Contact me quickly, only a few
know of our work, and even fewer do I truly trust anymore.

  Signed Dr. N. Jansen

"Nadene! Oh, it has been so long since I have heard from her."

"Wait, Aunty Nada?"

"Yes, one in the same, she and I used to work together and many digs, remember? We worked in graduate school together and many years and projects later."

  "I remember you took me on a number of digs during the summer months, never some place tropical, always the desert." Alena cracked a sarcastic smile as she found the file. Her mother had placed it in the bookshelf, probably to keep it away from Buddy's mouth. "Well, check your email and go for it, it is time you got back to the field, you loved your work, it was only second to me and dad."

  "You know, you're right and if it is the dig, I think it is then we are both going. It's odd though, this letter was sent priority. Postage was only three days ago."

With genuine curiosity, "You don't mean the librarians?"

"Yes, the Librarian and the remnants of the Library"

"But that is your life work, you've been looking for her, and have searched everywhere."

"I was looking in the wrong places, I never thought to look in one place, and now it seems so obvious!" Alexandria said impassioned with years of research finally bringing forward an answer. She walked to her bookshelves, laptop in hand, in the living room. Behind the couch there were two books shelves, Alexandria pulled on a book titled *The History of the Library: A theory of the truth;* it was her thesis. This book was published years ago and even republished into commercial reading circles. The it caused in the academic world was so thunderous.

Dr. Alexandria Martin was not a known archaeologist in any circle until she was working in graduate school on a theory. This theory was based on years of research prior to her entering academic circles. Her research involved the idea that the Library of Alexandria survived. Not the building itself, but all the documents and books due to a small group of select individuals that were entrusted with the very secret task to protect all knowledge. They were based in Alexandria, Egypt. Her research took years and many documents that were never translated from an ancient dialect of Greek. This dialect was difficult to read because parts, like many ancient documents, were missing but also due to its rare usage. This dialect was only used by those that could read it. It was a coded language, never spoken and only written. Alexandria was able to decipher it with great difficulty and kept her research, after publishing her basic theory in her thesis, secret. She was able to find the secret documents that led to the discovery of the secret knowledge keepers.

These papers she kept copies of, as the originals are not only fragile but limited access is allowed. Even that access is extremely difficult to gain. She petitioned for years to be granted access to these documents from who she thought were the individuals who housed them as private sellers. But this group was such a well-kept secret that even these private sellers didn't know what they had; they were a front to protect the real owners. People that are never seen.

Alexandria stepped out of the way as the book case moved backwards into the wall with a great thud. She walked through and when Alena didn't follow, she popped her head back, "Ala, it's okay it's my study."

Alena was cautious but followed suit, as she walked through the space that housed the bookshelf that was now acting as a door to a different world. The room was much bigger than the house allowed an outsider to think. There were bookshelves lining the huge room, it must have been the length of the whole house. She had lived in this house for seventeen years until she moved out, how did she not know about this room, she wondered. There was a grand old desk in the middle of the room, with a computer and papers everywhere. Ancient and modern maps hung all over the walls, but all of the same region of the earth: The Middle East.

The room smelled of aged paper and warm leather. The smell of an adventure ready to begin. The lighting was sufficient, not bright or dim, but it was enough to read the scrolls as well as to cause a little damage to the documents as possible. Alena had the sense that she had stepped into an archive deep beneath the world without a window or sense of natural light. Alena Martin hadn't realized that her breath had caught. The smell was so strong that it penetrated into a taste of her tongue. The taste was very subtle, like an after taste of the glue on envelopes. It wasn't unpleasant but not exactly a desired taste either. She didn't want to blink for fear that it was a dream. Turning her head, she absorbed as much as she could. "How did I miss this?" Alena whispered under her breath.

She had never seen so many ancient manuscripts before in her life, at least none so well preserved. There were two grand lamps at the desk and low lighting through the rest of the room. As she stood there, a few yards from the desk, she realized what this room reminded her of—it was a personal library built and dedicated to one topic. It was her mother's research to the first female librarian of the first unified library: Hypatia of the Library of Alexandria.

Chapter VII

James Benakis sat patiently in his study staring at the files that he had poured over so many times before. Again he sat praying that there was something new, something he had missed. But his younger sister was still gone without a trace. His sisters had gone long before their time. His parents had never recovered from the loss of the first, and when his remaining sister was killed in a tragic assassination, his father's grief consumed him. He died of a heart attack only six months after his sister and his step-mother died just a few years ago. Through all this, for some unfathomable reason, he still believed his sister was only missing and not dead.

He made it his mission to find her, he had her cold case unearthed. With the money he had left from his father and a wealthy family inheritance in the technology and oil investments he had built through the years, he wanted to find her. He was dying. He wanted to make sure that what was left of the family stayed in the family. He made a few phone calls to find out where he could find a Private

Investigator, or a boredom detective willing to take pity on a dying man. She had been last seen in Los Angeles, so that's where he started. She had been on a trip visiting a friend of hers, while at university. At the time it was a perfectly normal thing. Her family knew where she was, she wrote back home to England with regularity, but suddenly the letters and phone calls stopped. Then the news cycle aired on the home television that through the family for a whirlwind. He still remembered the words: "Young woman of prominent English political family missing, friend reported when she never showed for classes." The news anchor had said.

His father didn't understand, she had left from her university holiday visit in England just days before this report. Her friend was picking her up early from the airport to have a couple days before her studies picked back up. James was twenty-four years old at the time. The search was on. He remembers the hours that his father, the politician and business man, had spent of the phone trying to find her.

He couldn't do anything, helpless against the tragedy. Both James and his father did everything within their power to find her. It couldn't erase the loss, or guilt. James was the oldest, he should have protected her. He didn't know how he would given the situation, but that didn't stop the thought. He knew after years that it truly wasn't his fault, but he never forgot or forgave himself. The guilt was always at the back of his mind.

The case file was closed officially after a few years had gone by. They mourned their loss, James and his remaining sister Mariana, never gave up. Mariana even went to the same university as Adara for her graduate studies in international law. She followed her father into politics and became a respected ambassador for the English government. James had followed his father on the business end. Mariana got married and stepped out of the political sphere for a bit of time to raise her daughter. But the last time he heard from her was a strange phone call. James remembers it well enough:

"James, I don't have much time, I am sorry to call so late."

He rolled over so that his wife couldn't hear him whisper, "It's okay, Maria, is something wrong?"

"Well, not exactly, just important, something I should have told you a long time ago. I –" and the phone line cut off, but not before he heard a strangely muted sound, like a hiss and then a thudded puncture.

That was the last time he had heard her voice. The next time he saw her was at the family's Greek Orthodox church, lying in a casket. He tried to remember her face, it was twenty plus years ago now. She was so young, both she and her husband were shot and killed. Assassinated for their role in negotiating a peace treaty to end the threat of nuclear war in the east somewhere. The assassin was arrested, as a fanatic in an unnamed religious cult, saying that the world would be consumed in fire if we didn't protect ourselves with the weapons given to us. There was little satisfaction to be had after the arrest. The accused was killed in a fight in his holding cell, he didn't even make it to the trial. Even so, the whole ordeal of his sisters felt off somehow, something just felt as though it was missing. The last time he had seen his niece she was a babe in the arms of a man he didn't know. When introduced, he said that he was her uncle. He was too numb to truly inquire into it, and he was grateful that she had family to grow up with. Over the years he meant to reach out, but time slipped away from him.

After allowing himself to grieve, he didn't stop living his life merely kept their memory alive, by never giving up on finding the answers.

James lived a healthy life and was grateful for what he had. James Benakis had married the love of his life, Blanche Arthur. She was the classiest lady he had ever known. Always polite in public but she knew when and how to give an insult without the person ever knowing.

Blanche was beautiful, smart and funny. She was his best friend. They had met while at university at Strathclyde. She had actually rejected his advances and the first time he asked her out. It took two dozen roses and a second request on his knee to get her to say yes. But once she did, they were in separable. Blanche wanted for nothing, James made sure of it. She was a woman of great taste with a nose for a sale. He remembered the one regret she had, the one regret they shared. They never became parents. She was not able to have children after a lengthy bout with cancer in her early thirties, just after they had said their vows. She lived but was robbed of motherhood, she never fully recovered from it, but he loved her no less than the day he had fallen for her. She had died a few years ago during her second round of cancer. The last thing she said was she was sorry.

He missed her. Plain and simple. The house needed the vibrant presence she had no matter what she was doing. Flowers didn't even smell the same way without her. What he missed most of all was hearing her voice while he held her in his arms. He would soon join her, though it was a bittersweet thought. He had so much yet to do before time caught up with him.

James needed an answer to his life-long project. He had called several private investigators, even journalists for a unique perspective, but no new answers. Years would go

by in between his renewed attempts and it was during one
of these hiatuses, only six months ago, that he was the one
to receive a phone call.

"Hello?"

"Is this James Benakis?" a male voice asked.

"This is he, and to whom am I speaking?" he
cautiously responded.

"You can call me Kristos, I must apologize but I
may have some information on your sisters." The voice
said cryptically.

"How do you know them, and what kind of
information?"

"A photograph really, I am faxing it to you now,"

"Faxing—" but he was interrupted by his fax
machine.

"We will be in touch."

The phone went dead, the voice gone, and his
sisters' mystery only grew when he saw the photo. It was a
faded color photo. The car in the photograph was his sister
Mariana's but there were four people in the car, instead of
the reported total of three; the driver, his sister, and her
husband. There was another woman with something in her
arms. He couldn't make out the face or what was in her
arms, only that it indeed was new information.

With this new information he fervently made phone calls, but only one person picked up the phone, a younger man in his late twenties, "Hello?"

"Is this, um, Nick Inigo, the news journalist?"

"Yes, this is, how did you get this number?"

"Sir, it is listed on your newspaper's website. You're located in Los Angeles, yes?"

"Oh, yea, right, I forgot they had done that." He muttered, clearing his throat and then speaking again "For parts of the year, yes, when I am not working in the field."

"What is it that you specialize in?"

"Well, crime actually, why?"

"Good, I was hoping you could help me on something. I am looking to employ the services of an assistant or investigator of sorts. I am a relative of the victim of a cold case, that I do not believe should have been closed."

"Oh, I see," Nick said as he quickly wrote down notes for perhaps a story later. "Well, if it is unsolved and if the location of the crime was in fact in Los Angeles then the best individuals to call is actually the police department of LA."

"Thank you, I will."

"Have a good one sir, and good luck!"

The phone went dead mid-sentence. Nick hung up the phone and blew off the phone call as nothing more than someone mourning family that he never got over. But just in case he shot off a quick email to the Captain of the Robbery Homicide division of the LAPD, giving her a heads up on the phone call. She responded minutes later saying thanks for not only the heads up but for pointing the gentleman in the right direction.

James Benakis picked up the phone he had just placed on the receiver, he hated cell-phones and rarely used his except for business or travel, if he was at home, he used his landline. He looked up the number for the LAPD Special Operations Unit, then remembered to dial the country code and then the full phone number. Gratefully, he remembered his time differences, so he could be accurate within a couple hours. He was on London time, as that was home, and resided in the only remaining family estate. After a quiet a bit of the run-a-round, and repeatedly explaining who he is and what he was talking about and who he wanted to talk to, he managed to get to someone near the top of the hierarchy. The Captain in the Robbery Homicide division at the LAPD picked up. On the end of the line after a couple of tones, a rather attractive female voice started the conversation.

"Central Headquarters, LAPD Homicide, Captain Barton."

"Hello, my name is James Benakis, I believe you have jurisdiction over a thirty-five-year-old cold case that I would like to be solved."

"That depends, sir, what is the name of the victim or do you know the leading officer?" she calmly asked.

"I know the victim, she was my sister, Adara Benakis. She was a university student who went missing thirty years ago,"

"The daughter of the English politician," There was a pause, a slight rustle of pages, "that was an unsolved cold case, I was briefly studied the case in my academy days. I'm familiar with it, but, sir, it's been cold for thirty-five years. Why do you want it reexamined now?"

"I am dying, and I want a solved case before I leave this world, I want the truth about what happened."

"I understand sir, but what do you want me to do about it, I do not have an endless supply of detectives, I am tryin' to solve cases before they get cold." He could sense that she was truly trying to help but couldn't just drop everything and solve this.

"Captain, as a dying man's wish, can you please find your best detective, assign the case to them, please. I would like to donate some funds to the force that put so much time and effort into trying to find her in the first place, a gift to those that sacrifice their lives to protect people." He paused. Taking a sip of water from the small glass on his desk, clearing his throat before continuing "It's nothing more than a donation. I do, understand your situation as a business owner and as a human. But I just would like answers before that headstone sits six feet above me."

There was a beat "Sir—"

"Captain, it's not a bribe, it's a donation, I will write the check out and send it in the mail tomorrow, even if you say no, but I am hoping that you would like this case solved too. We must find the answers so that justice and what is good in this world can endure. So, do I have your yes?"

"I cannot guarantee anything, sir, but I did just remember one person that I can in fact put on the task."

"That is all I ask. The donation will be sent to the Central LAPD Robbery Homicide unit, and Captain…?"

"Yes?" The femininity hard to disguise though her tone was stern.

"Thank you." He hung up the phone before she had the time to say anything further. He felt a release as he went to his briefcase and wrote a check of a large sum for the donation and then wrote specific instructions to be sent to whomsoever would be assigned to the case to contact him if they ever needed a guiding hand or additional information.

Chapter VIII

Though the room was large and spacious one could smell the musty and aged pages of the manuscripts, as though the air was recycled through a museum-quality filtration. The pages and maps were so well-preserved she dared to wonder how they were transported here, or for that matter even found. The maps were for the vast majority, ancient with only a few modern maps for comparison. The shelves surrounded the room with large tomes and scrolls scattered in between. There were a pair of white preservation gloves on the desk next a large glass bubble; an old-style magnifying glass.

Alexandria placed her laptop on the desk, in the only open space on the wooden top, and plugged it in to the cord that was resting in the space. She booted up the computer as Alena stared at the maps and smelled that strangely comforting smell of old pages. Within a few minutes of silence, except for the light tapping of computer keys, Alexandria Martin found the email sent to her from Dr. Nadene Jansen.

"I didn't even know this place existed, I didn't know you actually had all of these documents."

"Not many people do, and you wouldn't have known how to get in yet, the code exists in two places—my head and my will."

"What do you mean?"

"These documents are secrets of the past. I never made the discovery public. I have them to protect and to continue with my research. But otherwise, technically, no one knows they are anything more than rumors of the past. Believed to have existed at one point but lost and the information on the scrolls only speculated at." She smiled.

"So, my mother is a modern-day Indiana Jones," Alena turned towards her mother with a light chuckle, "but why so secret?"

"Well, like any discovery, big or small, can have unknown impacts," As she continued to read the email, "I was simply trying to wade out and have all my bases covered before I drop any historical bombs, like I think it will."

"Hypatia as the first female librarian, this would be a historical bomb?"

"Well, yes, think about it, while I finish reading this email…" Alexandria pulled her hair away from her face and through a hair tie. She picked up the reading glasses on the desk, adjusting them to see through the bifocals without moving her head.

Without responding she did just that. Alena could see some complications like Woman's Rights groups and putting Hypatia at a more martyr for knowledge type than she already was but trying to find anything else was making it kind of difficult to see.

"I still don't understand."

Her mother stopped reading and turned towards her, this knowing look in her eyes. She loved to explain all the nuances involved in history. Alena knew she missed giving lectures. "Hypatia is believed to be more of a translator and commentator of knowledge than an innovator herself; however, in order to do either one must have an intimate knowledge in order to breakdown the information so that new learners can digest and understand the knowledge."

"I am listening," as she started to stare again at the map of ancient Alexandria, so beautifully detailed. The color faded away with time, but hints of the luxurious ink pigments could still be seen if she focused long enough.

"Hypatia and her father were known to be incredibly well-educated even for philosophers and mathematicians of the day because they read and knew so much, they could see and comment on the interconnectivity of all knowledge." Dr. Martin was getting more animated as she discussed it further, "They didn't necessarily change the knowledge like many scholars thought for years. No, they did so much more than that. They protected it, preserved it, copied it when needed, and translated. What modern day job description does that sound like to you?"

"An archivist."

"A librarian. A librarian would be more apt for the times. Hypatia was the first recorded female librarian. But a librarian of which library one might be thinking: The Library of Alexandria."

"But the Library of Alexandria was burned in the 4th Century BCE and the daughter library was destroyed a couple hundred years later during one of the many purges of knowledge by ancient Christians against the pagan religions of the time. Long before Hypatia was even born."

"I am glad you remember your conventional history dates, but those are in particular are wrong."

Alena turned from the map and began to ask a question when her mother's notification for another email went off. There was a quick tap from her mother's fingers. Alena made the short distance between the wall and the desk with a few steps. She looked at her mother with a voiceless nudge that her mother knew well—*Show me.*

Alexandria opened the new email. It was of the image of an old cut out cipher, the kind that could have been made of copper or another soft metal and were used on pages to find letters instead of words. No words were in the dialogue box except *Read again.* Alexandria opened the first email, the original sent by Dr. Jansen. Alexandria absentmindedly put her glasses on top of her head. She hit the print button, as it printed, she flipped back to the second email, but just as clueless as when she saw it the first time. Alena looked at it again and studied it. She noticed something. It looked like a number and a word but couldn't quite make it out.

"Mum blow this image up and print it off," Alexandria raised an eyebrow and waited patiently. Alena rolled her eyes, "Please,"

Alexandria nodded her head and smiled as she did so, she walked to the printer that was behind one of two bookshelves that acted as functional room-dividers. Dr. Martin came back to the desk reaching and then looking for something. Alena stopped her mother and pointed to her head. Alexandria grabbed her reading glasses, that constantly went "missing", from the top of her head. Alena placed the glass bubble on to the image. She focused the image and clearly saw the little smudges in what would have been the holes in the photographed cipher. She knew the symbols meant something but didn't recognize them.

"What are they?" she handed the glass bubble to her mother, who was now looking through two lenses. Alena grabbed the printed letter from Dr. Jansen. She wanted to read it quickly, until she got about half way through the second paragraph, when it started to dawn on her what it read, then she read it out load to confirm what she was reading:

> "'Hello, my dear friend, it has been far too long since we have seen each other. I cannot risk this information in any conventional message. Other than after you figure it out send back an email I am waiting. You should know by now that the funding not only went through but was doubled. Our mysterious benefactors have funded us indefinitely. I still do not know really who they are only that the individual who picks up the phone continues to do so and asks very few questions.
>
> They gave me a phone call after a mysterious email claiming to be the Keepers of Knowledge. From what information I was able to dig up on them, they are a very well-kept and quiet organization that funds many projects, anonymously for the most part. I am unsure as to how benign they are, or their true intentions in funding our research other than they want us to keep digging.

TEA TIME

*These Keepers have evidently existed for
some time, funding mostly archaeological digs on
controversial history, almost as though they are
trying to change history as it is written into
something slightly different. They fund many facets
in research across all fields of study, but no one,
that I have been able to talk to about it, has met
anyone claiming to be a Keeper. Only email and
phone calls.*

*It is very strange, but I need your help and I
need you to meet me. I truly can only trust you and
your daughter with this knowledge. Remember what
we used to say in grad school?*

When all trust is gone,
Look to yourself,
leave no stone unturned
experiences for One line will tell all
breathe in ancient air
one last time look behind
before your neck snaps back forward
Science and Math blended
This is a trusted keeper of Knowledge

My friend, I trust you to find me.

Alena read it over again, and still couldn't find anything significant but the poem. Her criminology experience told her it was important, but she would need a clue or a cipher to understand it. The cipher—now she understood to keep the key and the message separate. She looked back to the bubble again, but she still didn't recognize the symbols. She sighed in frustration and sat thinking at the desk, not seeing her mother's face light up.

Alexandria walked to the front of the room and began searching, mumbling under breath. "it's here somewhere...I just reorganized this shelf...no, it's –ah there you are!"

"Was this message encrypted?"

"Yes, it was glad you were paying attention" still searching for something. Deep in thought she found it.

"What is it?" her head looked away from the curious puzzle in front of her as she looked to her mother's voice.

"My thesis!"

"Mum, this is hardly the time to be reviewing your paper for old research, we need to solve the puzzle."

"Ah, but we are, and it is the ideal time to look at the past, sometimes old research and the history of antiquity needs a fresh pair of eyes." She walked back to the lighted desk and opened the book. This was the original academically published copy of her thesis. The commercially published had been slightly edited for more layman terms. This had all of her original writing. "The poem is a code,"

"OH! I understand! The poem is the code, the photo is the cipher, and the thesis is …what?" Still puzzled Alena looked again at the photographed cipher. "It's a double code!"

"Exactly, you remembered well."

"One, I am guessing is to a place, the other is the knowledge that was too valuable to email." She smiled as she looked at the cipher again, there was in fact several numbers on it, one next to each strange symbol. "But which one is which?"

"That is what we have to find out. There are fewer symbols…these look familiar, but I am not sure why…" Alexandria looked closer "That's it!"

"What is?"

"The symbols, they're two symbols super-imposed on the one another. If you break them apart you get a mathematical symbol and an astrological symbol. These are the cipher for my thesis. The mathematical is hidden behind the astrological, because that is the true key. Every one of these mathematical symbols is also a mathematical constant"

"I get it, clever Aunty Nada. She used the symbols as one because Hypatia was known as a scholar for both astronomy and mathematics but spoke Greek hence the math being the hidden key, because astrology was even known by then to have developed in Egypt."

Alexandria looked closer and wrote each of the symbols down as the whole and broke them a part, so she could see what she was dealing with. Taken apart from each other they were common symbols. There were twenty-three symbols, two repeated that she needed to pay attention to:

Ω Ψ ϑ ⟨τ π⟩ μ β δ ζ θ ω γ Γ ϖ α φ η ⟨τ π⟩ ν Φ ψ χ

The astrological signs didn't repeat:

A b c d e f g h I j k l m n o p q r s t w x y

"Now to go grab that math encyclopedia your father bought for me as a joke, I never thought I would actually need it." Alexandria found each of the numerical equivalents to the symbol and then rounded up to the fourth decimal. "You see each letter has a value in the mathematical sense. These are some of the mathematical constants, the original values never change and as you can see some were developed or discovered by the Greeks, hence the symbols."

"I recognized pi," Alena pointed to the familiar symbol, "the value of the ratio of a circle's circumference in relation to its diameter also known as 3.1415."

"Exactly," Her mother smiled, "I am glad that private English education paid off,"

"Those uniforms didn't," Alena snickered as she remembered having to wear such a strict dress code. She was grateful to have left that uniform in England but keep the private education. "Why are you rounding?"

Alexandria pointed with her fountain pen, "Which part of the book, which Page, Paragraph, sentence, and finally word."

Alena shook her head, codes never ceased to fascinate her. Her cipher for the poem was much simpler, one number per word with a hyphen and one number per letter, like a date without a year. The Cipher image was the clue for that. Alena wrote down each of the numbers and looked back at the poem. Each number she double-checked to ensure that it was in fact the correct letter. A number for the line, represented by the hole's placement on the cipher, the image for the cipher was just another key to the numbers written that represent the word and letter within that word this pattern. The pattern was slow to immerge, but she was patient. The code showed itself. Clues given began illuminating within the spaces of the code. She wrote a letter down in pencil, in case she had to change it. The code numbers were simple but effective:

1-2-1, 2-1-1, 3-3-5, 4-1-2, 4-7-1, 5-3-2, 6-5-6, 7-2-4, 8-1-3, 9-3-1

Alena wrote down the numbers and then wrote down the letters that were equivalent to the numbers, and sure enough the name of a place began to appear.

"Any luck with your decoding skills?"

"They're a bit rusty, but I have my message." Alena smiled, she did have a shorter message to decipher, but she double checked it anyway.

"I finally have mine." Dr. Martin said in a decided manner, grateful she kept that joke from her husband on her shelves. "the message is short words, like a telegraph style. Hypatia—Buried—Library—Alexandria—Murder—Has—More—Than—Stone—Knowledge—Keepers—Organised—Librarians—Copied—All—Documents—Library—Alexandria—Not—Destroyed—Buried—Help"

"I guess we are packing out bags and finding a Buddy sitter. My message had one word: Alexandria."

Chapter IX

Though the day was still young, the sun's heat was enough to make a person wish for rain. The dig site was the result of years of research, funds and hope that this was the right site. This was not the first hunt for the Library of Alexandria, but it was one of the few modern searches. Dr. Jansen and Dr. Martin had teamed up years ago as their research and goal was similar: to find the scrolls of Alexandria. The wealth of knowledge that was lost in time with the library is unfathomable. The two women believed that the first female librarian was also a protector of sorts. This librarian, according to their research, was Hypatia, the well-known commentator and teacher of the Hellenistic age.

Years of research, negotiations and back tracking went into the time to get permission for countless organizations, countries and antiquities council for this dig site. Then the after the permission was granted, funding had to be acquired, additional researchers called, and a team created. More time, more research, thousands of emails between Dr. Alexandria Martin and Dr. Nadene Jansen sent.

Checks, double-checks, revisions, and proposals sent, rejected for funding. Backers wanting more information and both women trying to find a way to give it without revealing their sources. The many sources were a ground-breaking discovery in and of itself, but needed to wait until it was safe to reveal the documents. They had been properly authenticated but Dr. Martin wanted to wait for the reveal until they proved the theory that they were a part of the missing Library. Meeting after meeting, so much time was invested into gathering funding. Dr. Jansen was always better at that than Dr. Martin, so Dr. Martin left her in charge of the project when her husband fell ill. She hadn't returned officially to the project until Dr. Nadene sent the message.

Dr. Nadene Jansen needed her friend, now more than ever. One of her team members was missing and the local police force hadn't done anything more than take a missing person's report. She knew it wasn't going to go anywhere, but she needed to put it on file. If Sita Richards did not reappear, she would have to call the embassy or someone with a higher authority to find her. Trying to breathe and stay calm until her friend came was her ultimate priority.

The dig had to remain her priority, with the hope that Sita had simply forgotten to call in the back of her mind. She had received a not stating Sita, wasn't feeling well, but her roommate didn't remember coming in the night before. It had felt off, leaving Dr. Jansen to make the report to the police.

Nadene breathed in and out, repeating the motion until she could no longer hear her heart in her ears. She needed to focus on her work. Grateful, that only a few people in the world knew the full details of the dig, she looked over the documents she had made available to the team.

Aside from a number of documents that mentioned her in the library often they had no real proof that their hypothesis was even able to be proven. Peter walked in to the tent and started to examine the documents. The tent was a make-shift study with documents on top of a desk made out of the boxes put into a compactable desk frame. It was a custom design by Dr. Jansen herself. Peter was unaware of the details but needed to garner something, maybe they slipped up and wrote a note or there was new or added information into the mix. There wasn't. With his lack of genuine knowledge of the particulars any new information, actually being missed was entirely possible.

"Peter, come I need you to do something for me."

"Yes, Dr. Jansen?"

"I need you to keep working." Said a blonde woman in her late fifties, but aside from a touch of grey, right at the roots, one would never guess. The woman was fit, and beautiful. Her hair was short and well-kept, beneath a blue and damp bandana. She was in a pair of old dusty denim pants and light-weight long sleeved shirt made out of the fabric that wicks away moisture. Her combat style boots crunched the compacted sand beneath her feet as she walked back to the small table beneath the tent that was used as their hub for research. She walked out of the document tent and to the one to the east.

The sun was blazing on the outskirts of Alexandria. They were not in the city but just outside of the city limits. Alexandria was different than most of Egypt. As it was in ancient times it was a coastal city, with only of the only places of green earth in Egypt. Unfortunately, with each passing year and climate change being no friend to the coast, the sands of Egypt were overtaking parts of the city. Parts of the ancient city lay miles from the current city buried between layers of earth and the sands of time. The site they were working on was on such site, past the modern city and into the green beneath a few layers of sand and earth.

She quickly opened the tent flap and caught a moment of relief from the heat. The tent was about ten degrees cooler. The maps were rolled out and paperwork held down by rocks of limestone. She flipped up the lenses of her sunglasses to check her computer screen. She hadn't told anyone that she had sent the information to Dr. Martin, she didn't want anyone to know. She had been warned in an email with the Knowledge Keepers symbol that someone near her, at her dig site, was not to be trusted with anything.

She saw that a message had been added to her inbox. It was from Alex with only two words, but she knew the code well: *Two Chariot.*

***

Peter walked back to the small square of dust he had been working on for days. He was not actually working but waiting for any sign that the dig would be called to an end. When it didn't, he'd had to get a plan approved by his superiors to expedite the plan. His new employers were a new breed of people he hadn't ever dealt with in life. Years ago, he had been dropped off at an orphanage in England. He was tossed around the first five years from foster parent to foster parent. Then a lovely interethnic couple, she was a teacher and he was a banker, adopted him to be the big brother for their three-year-old daughter, Sonja. She was a ray of sunshine, a blimp of joy in his life. They were only two years apart and he loved being a big brother. They started school at the same school, granted he was older and in first grade, but he got to see his little sister throughout the day. He remembered that time with sweet fondness. A soothing solace to his soul, that once he knew what it was life to be loved by a real family. To feel and be truly wanted. But it was short-lived.

The parents were killed in an accident when he was twelve, Sonja was ten. She went to live with an aunt and he was sent back to the foster system. The new adults in his life were okay, but he always felt out of sorts. They were an older couple in their late forties and set in their ways. It gave Peter an odd freedom, independence. He was often left to his own devices after being left in this new foster house. Forcing him to rely on no one but himself, he learned early on to not trust anything or anyone but himself. Peter learned to be alone and slowly he forgot what that warm feeling of a loving family was. He knew what it felt like to be somewhat forgotten, to be alone in a crowd. Peter's true comfort was spending time with Sonja at school. They were very lucky that they remained at the same school. It was an escape from the silence at the house and a chance to feel that warm feeling of being with a loved one. He was able to learn in school with Sonja and help her with school work as well. Despite being two years apart they shared a library period and they took full advantage of this oddity. They had a designated corner that they would meet every library period.

The library wasn't huge or anything fancy but it was their space. There was a window space by the fiction shelves that had pillows and chairs set up to be a reading corner of sorts with a little table, their space. He loved reading with her. It reminded him of when he was able to call himself a brother. This went on for years, Peter even skipped a couple of classes to be with her when his library period changed times. It went on as their routine for years until she got sick. His little sister was sick and there was nothing he could do but try to ease the pain. He visited her on her bad days after school, or on the really bad days in the hospital. He would bring her books to read to her and help with her homework. Sonja's worst day she was so weak he just held her and let her rest in his arms. Once the doctors were finally able to find a treatment that worked, Sonja slowly but surely improved. She even graduated high school on time.

After years of living within a system that he hated he finally had enough money to at least move out and start on his own. He started taking classes for his degree after a year out of the house with the money he saved up. He was alone in his flat one evening when he received a phone call from a man claiming to be his father.

"Peter, I don't have any better way to say this other than I am your father, I would like you to come live with me and take over by business."

"You could have found me years ago, why now? I can't talk to you I have to study for exams." With that Peter hung up the phone. He thought nothing more of the conversation. I told himself that it was one of those money scams. But weeks later, he still couldn't stop thinking about it. He finished his associate degree that year, at the age of twenty-five, he got a job at a tech start up the following year after working odd jobs here and there for rent money. After five years of routine and tedious paperwork being his constant he realized the cubicle dead-end job that he was hired for was so much less than what he wanted, despite the pay. The routine was not only tiring but annoying, but why he continued for another several months was to save up and find a way out. That was when he got another phone call, from the same man:

"Peter, don't hang up…"

After a long pause, not knowing what to expect, he brought the phone back to his ear, "What? What do you want?"

Peter could heat the man breathe a sigh out at the microphone crackled a bit. "I would like to invite you to a gathering of colleagues. Your ticket is paid for and your time away from your job is already taken care of. Oh! and a suit is arriving for you at your front door in the next hour."

TEA TIME

"I—" but Peter didn't have time to respond as he heard the dial tone click. He ignored the phone call, until his doorbell rang. Peter walked the distance from his bedroom to the door of his apartment. Upon opening the door, he saw no one but sure enough there sat a box on the floormat that contained a suit.

The next morning, he was on a flight to an estate in the heart of France. He wasn't sure what he was doing and almost didn't make the flight. Peter wanted to get away from work but he was thinking more of a visit to Sonja in Oregon. He had been thinking about surprising her for her finals. She was at university for creative writing. A trip to France to meet a bunch of old men and a man who called himself his father wasn't exactly his idea of fun.

He flew on a commercial flight to London but when he looked for the other gate numbers for his flight to Paris, he couldn't find it. A man dressed in pilot's uniform approached him. He asked his name and said to follow him. Peter thought he had left something on the plane, but then realized that a pilot wouldn't come track him down. They walked to a different side of the airport, passing several security points all with clearance levels that the pilot cleared, informing everyone he was a passenger who had gotten lost in transit. They both got into a car that was waiting for them and drove a short distance southwest of the airport. Peter thought he was in a dream. The driver didn't stop when they reached the airport, or pull into a parking lot, the driver cleared the entrance and instead he drove straight onto the tarmac. Sure enough, a small Cessna jet sat on the tarmac, primed and ready to be cleared.

The jet was simply luxurious. Peter took a seat buckled up and waited for take-off. A male steward came through offering a drink, he had champagne and a whiskey-neat on a small platter. Peter lifted the whiskey with a nod and smile. This was nice but his nerves were making him very uncomfortable. He needed to steel his emotions before they landed. Not more than thirty minutes after take-off, a beautiful and old chateau appeared. He finished the liquid courage as they prepared to land. Another car waited for him at the hangar that from the air looked about six to seven miles from the chateau. The car was another luxurious vehicle. It wasn't just any car with leather seats, it was a Rolls Royce Wraith in black. This was a clear show of money and excess. It was a whole other world that he had just stepped into. Peter never felt any rider smoother than this, he let himself enjoy the brief ride to the chateau.

He was dressed in navy, a pinstriped silk suit that came in the box. The Italian leather Oxfords that his foster father had given him for the last birthday they celebrated. It was one of the best gifts he'd ever received. The car door swung open without him realizing it. Without a word he got out and walked up and through the gate. Peter wasn't one to typically admire architecture, but this building was extraordinary. He got to the green front double doors and stood there. He took a moment to straighten himself and to breathe in. After a beat he raised a fist to knock but the door swung open before he contacted the wood.

"Master, Peter, come in sir. Your Father is waiting in the parlor." Said The man holding the door. He was dressed in black and white and was aging but distinguished no less. He bowed his head ever so slightly and walked through the door. The man pointed with an open hand in the direction of the room to the far back, behind the massive staircase. The house was either a family estate or cost the owner a fortune as the detail was immeasurable.

"Come, Peter, join me for a glass." That voice. The man that it belonged to was in a suit surrounded by a small group of other men wearing suits. Some of the men were in the basic black with the fitted jackets, a couple wore dark colors in near-black jewel tones, a few had very thin pinstripes on their suits. A pleasant mix of attire that seemed to match each man. Each suit was worth more than Peter would make in two years. These men had power and money and it showed. Power and money were like breathing and water to these men. There was something else going on here, this meeting was more than simply power.

These were not simply businessmen. These were the men in power behind the scenes of every business and government, the men behind the curtain as it were. Everyone knew they existed, but they only showed themselves when and if they chose. Never would he be in a room like this again. The man who claimed to be his father looked like a dashing actor from the 1940's; his hair was gelled back with a gentle wave to its darkness, a thin mustache but otherwise clean-shaven, his suit pressed and sharp in a deep shade of indigo with faint pinstripes of dark grey. He looked barely old enough to be a father let alone his, but if there was one thing Peter had learned it was that appearances can and often are deceiving.

Peter stopped at the doorway and looked around the men in the room were of different ethnicities, all but a few were not much older than fifty. He looked back again to the man that had beckoned and noticed the white hair beginning to show at his temple and just beneath his nose on his mustache. He held a glass of red wine in his hand and offered a glass to Peter with the other. Peter accepted the glass.

"Thank you." Peter said quietly.

"Of course," The man claiming to be his father said. But instead of moving back like Peter anticipated, he moved in closer and he stayed there for a moment, whispered, "I will explain everything" Peter could smell the sandalwood scent of his after-shave with a tinge of the sweet alcohol from the wine mix on the man's breath. Peter nodded his head ever so subtly.

Peter stepped back politely as the men raised their glasses, "To the true Keepers of Knowledge." Every man took a healthy sip from the elegant, clear crystalline glasses and paused for a moment as though each were in contemplation of something. Slowly a hum rose and then the small talk resumed as though there had never been any interruption.

***

Peter walked outside to the balcony that was just beyond the French doors of the parlor room where the gathering was being held. The glass doors muted the sounds of the gathering. He was alone, for the first time that day. Grateful for the silence he breathed in the night. He stood there and tried to unravel what this day was. He was finally meeting his father, his biological father. But where was his mother, he wondered. All his life people had

106

been abandoning him. His parents from the day he was born. Each foster family he stayed with didn't want him, his friends when a family finally decided to keep him. He was six when he was officially adopted. Six years and eight different schools, he was always the "new kid" "the unwanted boy" "the foster kid". The only person who called him by his name was generally the teachers. Once or twice though, he had heard the teachers refer to him as "the poor foster child" when it was just the adults.

His friends at the orphanage saw him every couple of months when the parents returned him like a bad book. Once he was adopted his friends finally abandoned him. They would even talk to him at school. They were great people he loved them very much, enough that after a few months he'd actually started to call them "mom" and "dad". But it didn't last.

He was abandoned, left alone, again.

He was picked up the next morning, on his birthday, and put into another foster parents' care. Peter shut out most of the world after that. The thought that his parents would find him and wanted him left him in his teen years, but it was always there in the back of his mind. He still dreamed of meeting them and getting an answer why, the thought haunted him. What would he say or how would he even react to his parents, he wondered. Now was his chance.

"Peter?" The voice he had learn to think of as his father spoke, breaking his thoughts.

"Sorry, I am not much for crowds" Not even turning to face him.

"Well, I would like to explain a few things if you're willing to listen," he paused for a moment. "Let me properly introduce myself, I am William Pritcherson. But you may recognize my name as Bill Pritch, the quiet CEO of Pritch Technologies. I developed the RFID technology that is used today, yes, the common creator is someone Theremin. But I made it more compact and able to not only receive but send out signals. I was making a lot of money in the beginning of the company, when I met your mother."

"My mother?"

"Yes, we met here in France, she was at some conference with her political father, she was looking into studying international law at the time. I was here for a modern technologies conference. We met at the hotel we were staying at and had a cup of tea in the lounge together. Shortly after we started seeing each other."

"Well, what happened?" Peter turned his head to him, glad that he just cut to the chase and avoided the small talk.

"She got pregnant, as women do, she told me, and I said we needed to think over a few things, but before I could give her an answer she disappeared. I never heard from her again."

"Then how do you know I am your son," now genuinely confused, Peter tried to figure it out.

"Well, I kept track of any documents and was on the lookout any child by her last name. But none of the orphanages had a child to that name. So, for years, I worked to keep myself busy but kept an investigator on tab to keep looking. But the dumbest thing I did was never to look for a child with my name. I don't know why it took me so long to think of it. She put you under the name of Pretchisen. She had changed the spelling but it was still my last name. Probably to distance herself, though I am not sure why."

"I was not given a first name by her?"

"No, that was my doing, I asked them to name you Peter after my father, but they would not let me adopt you. They let me name you, but they wouldn't let me get near you."

"That's strange."

"Yes, but the point is that now we are here together at last, father and son."

Peter smiled for the first time in a long time, he liked the sound of that: father and son. He unbuttoned his jacket and looked at this man. For the first time someone was not only being kind to him and treating him as an equal, but he looked like him. This man, though a little lighter in skin color, and his eyes were more hazel than brown, looked like Peter. There was a genuine resemblance.

Both men were well-built, spending time in extensive exercises was a pass time for both men, rather attractive, and tall. They easily fit the tall, dark, and handsome description that women looked for in men across the globe. There was a smugness to the father that the son had not yet acquired, some would call it the look of a womanizer. Although, good-looking as he was, Peter had not had a lot of luck with women on a genuine relationship level, he saw them a pastime, nothing to keep around. The only female he'd had any kind of lasting relationship was his adopted sister.

"Why did you call me here, Bill?" Decidedly changing the subject.

"Well, I am not as young as I look, and I want to retire, but that means I need to pass down my affairs to someone else."

"Which I am guessing is where I come in?" asked Peter.

"Exactly, but you see it's not as simple as some paperwork, there is…training involved."

"Training?"

"Yes, you see I am not just a simple business man, I have two jobs. One that I gave myself with technology and one I was given in part because that technology."

"I am not sure that I follow?"

"Can I trust you?"

A little more than puzzled, but very intrigued Peter responded "yes."

***

That conversation changed his life, forever. His father was a member of an international form of a secret service for an organization simply referred to as the Regulator. This organization kept tabs on all available information no matter how minute. They were in control of the flow of information and knowledge available in the world at any given time. All religions had a member or two involved in this organization as do every business big enough to have influence in how the global society and stability operates, soda companies, car and big retail names were all represented among the ranks. With this kind of control, the information that the world sees was in their control. Only the information they wanted to be known was allowed beyond the doors. Vast pieces of history have been erased from modern history lessons, mathematics and sciences are controlled, the arts allow for too much creativity and are slowly being limited. Religion is allowed as it is controlled by the organizations, all religions, but they are also allowed to work against each other. The community of Regulator controls the flow of information and how it was used but not how people react to it. The original records of everything was stored in a secret location that even his father claimed not to know.

William Pritcherson was of a select group of men that had been trained in a multifaceted program to find and destroy any threat to the Regulator. He had also tried to convince Peter that it is best for society for information to be controlled and carefully evaluated before any piece was given to the masses. These men and this organization have existed in some form or another for centuries but had become stricter over the past couple of generations in their level of control. The appearance of the internet as a mass populace technology was a new challenge but also an incredible asset.

The fellow members, along with William Pritcherson, were men that rarely had big families, were all pillars of the community, and men in positions of power. They had been trained in martial arts, technologies, politics, and a variety of other subjects. This training was to allow these members to slip in and out of society undetected even by the governments. Their service was reconnaissance for the Regulator and in an emergency destroy any unwanted information without the world noticing any loss.

Peter was the newest member, by default as the son of a member, brought in. Peter was a rare instance of a second generation and had through careful cultivation been put through the training as a child and had continued much of it as an adult. His father had carefully, through discreet channels, had him take classes in the several subjects needed to become an ideal candidate for membership. That's why his foster parents allowed him to keep taking mixed martial arts, even though his teacher was across town. His teachers had helped him get into higher level courses and even college classes as a junior.

Peter was mostly complete with his training before he had even met his father. Without even realizing it he was in the club so to speak and didn't realize it until his father had explained everything that night. There was something that he was going to have to do, go back to school, to finish the training. Before peter protested, William told him that the organization was paying for it.

"That's a lot of information, to process," Peter stood quietly. "What subject am I studying?"

"Yes, it is, and I wished there were an easier way, but I have always been there for you, molding you into who you are. Oh, its not that kind of school but you will be attending a few classes on anthropology and archaeology until the Regulator sends you on your first mission."

"That may be, but you were not there for me."

"No, I wasn't, but I am now." Bill Pritch put his arm across his son's back, "And we have a lot to do."

Chapter X

Stevie walked up to the house that she visited many times during her university days. She had a bachelor's degree in creative writing but after a few years of trial and error books she decided it was time for a different perspective. She had met her best friend on the first day of her first year back to school. She was in her mid-twenties with what remained of her college fund for her bachelor's and an open perspective. Alena was a first-year freshman at the time studying Forensic Archaeology and criminology. Stevie was still undecided for her post graduate but was interested in a ton of subjects.

They were in an Anthropology 101 class, at UCLA. Alena wanted to be a forensic anthropologist, but unsure what she wanted to do with the degree. Dr. Jansen was their professor, she was in between dig seasons at the time. That first day, they were covering the evolutionary timeline of humans. Alena sat next to Stevie at the beginning of class, and every day after that. They shared a couple of classes and many common interests, becoming very fast friends.

"Hey, I got your call, don't worry I have your back."

"Thanks, Stevie, I owe you a bottle of your favorite and a bar of your favorite chocolate."

Stevie chuckled, "You know you don't have to do that, but you know what my favorites are if you want to." She grabbed her friends' bag and tucked it into the taxi sitting out front of the house. Alena had a backpack on her shoulders with a duffle bag in her hand. Dr. Martain had the two bags in hers, one of which looked on the verge of exploding. Stevie grabbed it and helped to put the rest in the truck of the taxi.

Alena handed Stevie the spare house key and got in the car with a Thank you. Stevie walked in to the house and sat on the couch with Buddy. There was a note on top of a pile folders.

Stevie,

Thanks for doing this favor for me, I am sure Buddy will be good for you and happy for your company. Even though, Mom and I are working on an assignment in Alexandria you can call, use the app and I will be working on the case as much as I can. I haven't really found anything new just in case you were wondering or even thinking about a new story. But as you know that doesn't mean anything.

Buddy eats twice a day. His food is in the fridge and if you run out, the recipe is in on the fridge. Treats are up in the cupboard. He will probably just sleep with you.

We are not sure as to how long we will be gone, but I'll stay in touch. You have my number, we are on an international plan so don't worry about calling. Oh, and if you need a car, mine is at my apartment, I left you the spare key. Take it to Jim, the mechanic on Olympic, he's a good friend and great with the old car, it's due for its annual, if you wouldn't mind too much. Any bill, just have him send it to me.

Thanks again my friend, Lots of Love And give me a buzz

Alena

"Oh Alena, always so polite" She smiled, as she scratched the ears of the little dog that had curled up to her leg.

Chapter XI

D r. Martin and Alena were seated in business class on the Delta flight to Alexandria, Egypt. It was going to be a long flight, so after placing their bags in the overhead bens, they quickly settled in. Dr. Martin was in the window seat, giving Alena a bit more space to work and making her claustrophobia ease back to crevasses of her mind.

Alena Martin pulled the case file out of her messenger bag, before placing it under the seat in front of her. She also grabbed her reading glasses and the legal pad in the back pocket. *Okay time to dig deep, I have hours to go through this, thought ought to get me familiar with the case if nothing else*, Alena thought as she opened the case file.

The thirty-five-year-old case had been cold for the vast majority of the time it was even filed. A young student from England, studying at UCLA had gone missing. She had last been seen by her family in England, but was supposed to arrive back from holiday to a friend's place in LA. The victim was twenty-five at the time, no criminal record, English and an American driver's license. She drove a family owned car while studying. The car had gone missing along with the girl. It looked like a runaway story. No note left, light packing perhaps. She had used a pseudonym on all her files and documentation at the university, which was a bit odd but understandable for the family she belonged to. The name was missing from the file. Her father was a prominent politician in England and didn't want to use that as a connection.

Alena made a note of that:

Pseudonym. Missing? Follow-up if possible.

They found the car a few years later, abandoned. The strange part was as though it had just been abandoned a few weeks before, it didn't have all the wear of a typical years-long-abandoned vehicle.

Freshly abandoned car? Killer/kidnapper kept the

car? Why? Victim's car in LA, did she make it?

What was she running from...or to?

There was one picture of the victim, but it was rather fuzzy and almost useless as the girl was much younger, but it gave her an idea. Maybe she could clean it up and age progress. *Later*, she thought, but she wrote it down anyway. There were pictures of the family home in England and the friend's house, her living space in LA, in an attempt to case it and find anything, but no one knew what to look for then and Alena was not sure what to look for now. The photos were all taken from a distance and poor quality. Time is hard to capture. The basics was all she could look for. Now, to look at her victim's relationships, if she had any. On the legal pad, she wrote:

There was the friend, the family, did she have a significant other? Friend called in the missing person's report...she doesn't have any obvious motivation.

Family was devastated when she went missing.

Step mother and Father no longer living, if they knew anything, I can't do anything about that.

What about the brother?

She continued to flip through the pages of the case, looking for any kind of information, even the smallest detail, but there really wasn't much to go on despite the number of documents in the manila folder. It was a very high-profile case, at the time, and became an international case given who the victim was and the simple fact that no one knew where she went missing to.

England or LA? Interpol?

Alena stopped for a second to gather her thoughts. She rubbed her eyes under her lenses and thought. She took her glasses off, rubbing the bridge of her nose as the elevation pressure was affecting the cabin. Sleep was creeping up on her. *What is the motivation?* According to the documents the victim didn't have a boyfriend of any kind. The Interpol file was truncated in the manila folder, which was the bulk of the paperwork. She looked to her note pad and realized she had less notes than what she normally did. Just goes to show that more paperwork doesn't necessarily get better results.

She had a few ideas what might be in here, but as she opened it, she would not have guessed she would have seen so much redacted. *Damn, I am going to have to call Interpol, after all. Especially, if I can't find anything from their scraps.* Alena flipped through trying to find more than fragments of a sentence. There was a better picture of the English family estate, underneath it says the estate stayed in the family and was inherited by the son. Gratefully, there was a bit more information on the brother, a name, James Benakis. He had gone into business as an investor and had done rather well. Interpol had even kept track of how often he had called their missing person's department or other agencies.

"Ma'am, would you like something?"

Alena breathed sharply, slightly startled. She was normally so aware of her surroundings. The young male flight attendant looked at her apologetically. "I didn't mean to startle you," He said quietly, noticing Dr. Martin was asleep with her headphones in. Alena could just hear Simon and Garfunkel coming into the stale air of the pressurized airplane.

"You didn't. I was just working,"

"Would you like anything?"

"Do you have a cuppa green tea? Hot?"

He nodded his head, "Anything for her?"

"Umm, I think it's an English tea with a touch of milk?"

"I can do that," He handed the green tea to Alena first. She hadn't realized how spread out she was. She had to carefully pop down the tray in front of her mother and place the teas there.

"Lunch order's will be taken shortly,"

"Thanks," Alena said without looking. Alena let the teas steep while she placed her legal pad, like a book mark, in between the pages of the folder. She couldn't help but think something was missing, a key piece of information. This case just didn't add up. She had a loving family, two siblings, friends, smart student with a bright future; Alena didn't want to think it was simply random. Her gut instinct was rarely wrong: something was off. She opened the file for Interpol again in hopes her cursory glance was just that. She looked that the photos and the documents. Nothing spoke to her so she closed the file. As she was putting the folder back in her bag, a small note fell out.

It was a bit bigger that a Post-it note and she recognized the handwriting. She had seen that shape of letters many times on her reports—the Captain. She picked it up and read it. The numbers were a phone number, an international number by the looks of it the country and area code. If she remembered from her days in England it was a number just outside London. There was a name penciled underneath, Bendakis.

"Mom, are you up?" Alena whispered when she heard a rustle from her mother.

With a short groan Alexandria Martin said, "Yes," She rubbed her neck and tried to stretch in her seat, "I smell tea,"

"Yea, yours should be strong enough, they're still hot," Alena picked up her tea and sipped gently noticing the barely-there steam.

"A good cuppa tea," Alexandria picked up the single use cup and let the warmth seep into her hands before she sipped.

Still staring at the phone number on the Post-it and the name. Bendakis, Alena knew this to be the only way to contact the only living relative of the victim: the brother. She would have to wait until they landed in Alexandria, still hours away. She sipped her tea and tried to think, with the hum of the airplane engines the only sound the broke the stale silence.

***

It was just another day on a sunbaked earth and sand bed of fine grain dust that reached every spot of the body. Every annoying spot. Kendra Michelle was so tired of this heat. She was one of several people involved in this dig in Alexandria. She was excavating one of the numerous squares that had been brushed and chiseled bit by bit. But this heat was exhausting.

Kendra got up very carefully and out of the square of space she was in. Her water bottle was in the shaded tent and she went to go grab it. She pulled her black curly hair up and it turned into a curly Brillo pad. She didn't bring any of her tools to straighten her thick frizzy hair, but she didn't care. She just wanted to drink her water. She was grateful that her skin was so naturally dark, thanks to her Caribbean parents. People said she didn't tan because she was already so dark. Kendra was just glad she never burned, but she wore sunscreen anyway. She was so warm; in fact, she unbuttoned the first button on her shirt in a vain attempt to cool offer. Kendra wanted to peel her skin off she was so uncomfortable in her skin. She knew how wrong that thought was, everything was sticking and wet with sweat. Her chest was a deep caramel color while her arms had gotten darker since being here. She hated the heat.

She had been working with the NYU department of Forensic Anthropology for a few years. She got the job when a friend in the department asked when the last time it was that she had worked in her field and not just studied it. She realized she had received her PhD five years ago and that was the last dig she had been on. She had always stayed in touch with her field, but it was hard to make it a living. She had been working with academics, lectures and student for so long. She started as a TA to one of her instructors as an undergrad and never really left. The pay was enough to afford her a one-bedroom apartment and dog, but little time for much else. Kendra Michelle was a very good and meticulous student and even more critical teacher. NYU offered her a position as a lecturer for undergraduate classes, teaching three classes a semester. That was during her Master's degree. She taught, researched, published, and graded like any good academic but she wanted a little more. She missed the thrill of being in the field. That was when she looked around for any digs that needed excavationists but got a call from Dr. Jansen instead, and the rest was history.

Now she wished she had air-conditioning. Kendra Michelle sat on the fold-out chair under the shaded tent until she began to cool off. Dr. Jansen walked into the tent. With a towel in her hand and her hat in the other. Her blonde hair was a bit damp from the sweat. She sighed and sat in the chair opposite Kendra.

"Dr. Jansen,"

"Dr. Michelle, I noticed you're a little dehydrated..."

"I just forgot how much water I used to drink on these desert digs."

127

"Yea, it always takes me a couple days to get acclimated."

"Yea, I'll be fine in a couple minutes." She took another sip of water.

"I appreciated you coming out, but I don't want you getting sick either. The day is almost over, so why don't you take the rest of the day and get some rest and rehydrate."

"Do I have a choice?"

"Not if you want to come back tomorrow." Dr. Jansen said with a smile.

"Okay then,"

"I will call for Peter. After Sita disappeared, I don't want anyone going anywhere alone. Check in when you get back to your room too, please."

"Alright, I appreciate this," Dr. Michelle was truly grateful and the longer she sat there the more she realized that Dr. Jansen's request was the accurate action. Dr. Jansen nodded and walked out of the tent calling for Peter. Dr. Michelle took another couple sips of water when Peter walked into the tent.

"Hey, Peter,"

"Dr. Kendra," There was a smile at his lips. Dr. Kendra Michelle had been greeted upon her arrival by Peter. He had picked her up and taken her to dinner the first night she was there. Later that night, though he was a little awkward, when he asked for her to come up to his room she didn't refuse.

"Thanks, Peter for taking care of Dr. Michelle,"

"Not a problem I'll make sure she gets back,"

Peter helped Dr. Michelle up from the chair and walked with her to the car that would take them back into the outskirts of Alexandria where they were staying at a local hotel. It was a simple and inexpensive place but better than sleeping on the sand. Dr. Kendra Michelle checked in, letting Dr. Jansen know that she was in her room with a gallon of water. After her meal and a shower, she quickly fell asleep.

When she didn't show up the next morning Dr. Jansen was a little concerned, even though Peter reassured her that Dr. Michelle had decided to hang back and rest up for today. But it was the next morning that caused Dr. Jansen more concern for her friend and colleague, without a word she disappeared. For the second time Dr. Jansen was on the phone with police and the Head of Antiquities at the museum in Alexandria that they were working with. Something was off, just like Sita Richards, one of Dr. Nadene Jansen's current students.

Dr. Jansen knew that sometimes while on a dig she would lose a couple excavators to the tourist side of the city, which was fine and encouraged, as long as they checked in with her. It was her responsibility to care and keep track of everyone, as the leader of this dig. But now she had two team members missing, and her best friend and partner was coming on to the dig with her daughter tomorrow. This was a dangerous problem.

Chapter XII

The landing wasn't as soft as Alena was hoping for but, at least they walked off the plane without missing any luggage or damages, unlike the several times she had flown to Denver International. As soon as she was comfortable with the placement of her bags, she and Dr. Martin walked to get the rest of their luggage.

The airport was like nothing Alena had seen before. It was so sleek and modern she felt as though she had landed in a classic sci-fi novel. Chrome was in every direction and reflected the halls, giving a disorientating feeling. It was so open for an airport. There was so much space, it felt as though the walkways were the size of airplane hangars themselves. Smaller than Atlanta by both number of people traveling but also in size, but it wasn't cramped with people like Atlanta International. It was so nice to not bump into someone as she tried to pass on the walkway. Alena heard countless dialects of Arabic among many other languages. It was all connected in one long terminal. She hadn't been this excited to be at a dig since her second dig in Greece in grad school. She had tested out of so many hours of classes that most of university time was grad school.

She pulled out her phone and turned off the airplane mode in hopes that there was signal in this metal building. After taking a few seconds to reconnect, and gaining service, she stopped at a chair to pull out that phone number. Her mother kept walking until after several paces she realized Alena wasn't there and turned around.

"What are you doing?"

"I have a phone call to make. You might want to call Nada and let her know we've landed. She might be sending a car."

"Don't worry its already taken care of. Do you—" Alexandria Martin saw the photograph of the house, peeking out of case file in Alena's hand and with difficulty suppressed her surprise, "Where did you get this?"

"It's a photograph of the last known sighting of the victim whose case I'm working on. Why, do you recognize it?"

Catching herself and clearing her throat she answered, "Just from the papers, I knew people who lived there," She tried to appear nonchalant.

Alena knew there was something off in the way her mother answered; however, now was not the time to push that button as to why but how she knew about this photo, she hoped the why would come later.

"What do you mean? What do you know about this house?"

"I can tell you only that I knew someone from there, but I don't know about a murder or any other death except that the youngest daughter died tragically. She and her husband were killed, the papers said that she was pregnant, and no one lived." After a brief pause, Alexandria said, "I don't want to talk about this, we need to catch our ride."

"Right, just let me get that other phone number,"

Alena grabbed the Post-it note piece of paper and pulled her phone out. She dialed the number and was grateful for her phone's battery life. As she waited for the phone to be picked up, she replaced the file into her bag and continued walking through the polished yet sterile airport.

***

James Bendakis was just finishing up an appointment with his doctor to check on his cancer treatment. Hormone therapy was the best option that he had at the moment. His doctor had said that it was going to have some side-effects but hopefully better than chemotherapy. He had Prostate cancer and was willing to try anything until he found his sister. His next refill was on its way to be picked up, as he rode away from the cold and sterile hospital room.

At the pharmacy while waiting in line, he felt his pants vibrate. He reached into his pocket and picked up his phone. James didn't recognize the number but decided to answer it anyway.

"Hello?" The voice on the other line said. It belonged to someone young and female that much he could tell. But what surprised him was how oddly familiar the voice was.

"Yes, who is this?"

"I apologize, I am looking for a James Benakis, I am Alena Martin. I believe my captain spoke to you and assigned me your sister's case."

This was the best news he had heard in such a long time, that he forgot he was at the pharmacy until the individual behind him kindly nudged him forward. "Yes, do you have anything new?"

"Actually sir, I was hoping to talk to you sometime soon, you see I am in Alexandria working on something right now. But I am also working on your case and just wanted you to know that."

"Well, thanks and I would like to talk further, but can this wait, I am in the middle of an errand." Not wanting to be rude to either the people in line nor the young detective making a long-distance call.

"Yes, just give me a buzz when you have the chance."

"Sure, okay then." She then hung up.

There was something familiar to the voice, but James couldn't quiet place it. He picked up his prescription distracted and almost forgot to sign for them. Why did she sound so familiar?

***

By the time Alena Martin had finished her phone call the two women were looking for a sign. The sign they never saw but they did hear their names. With a spin they saw who was calling: Nadene Jansen.

"Nadene, what are you doing here in person?" Alexandria asked a bit more than puzzled, "Isn't that normally for the interns?"

"Normally, yes, but this isn't a normal occasion."

135

TEA TIME

"I don't understand, what's going on?" Alena chimed in as she slipped her phone in her jacket pocket.

"I have two members of my team missing.

The Missing

Chapter XIII

"**M**issing?"

"Nada, you didn't say anything about anyone missing in your email." Alena stated, trying not to sound suspicious or alarmed.

"Because when I sent that information, only one girl *was,* and I just figured she had gone a bit native. After I called the cops and the museum partner for the dig. But she and one of my supervisor excavation experts, a friend, is now missing without a trace." Nadene stated quickly with a bit more that distress in her voice.

"Let's get to the car and tell us everything on the way," said Alexandria trying to take control of the situation.

They walked to the exit. Where the car sat in the parking lot. Alexandria got into the driver's seat, turning over the engine as she asked, getting straight to the point, "What is going on?"

Nadene breathed in and told everything that had happened since the beginning of this dig. The fact that these two women had "gone native" or more like "gone tourist", as the police were calling it, a bit longer than she thought was a growing concern. The fact that no one had heard from them was even more to worry about. Normal protocol requires that everyone involved contacts the leader of the dig, in this case Nadene, at the beginning and end of the day. Neither of these women had done so, the first to go missing was last heard from four days ago and the most recent was two days ago.

"There is an established pattern," Alena pointed out, "two women gone missing in four days, two days apart,"

"What are you saying, that someone is kidnapping my team?"

"It's not out of the realm of possibility, foreign country, foreign laws, most of your team is young, of different ethnicities, but mostly American educated, at least for their bachelor's degrees if not their post-graduate."

"She read that file and a lot of others on the way over here," Alexandria elaborated.

"Do you think they are dead?" concern swelled in Dr. Jansen's voice.

"Have any demands been made?"

"No, none that I am aware of."

"That's good for now, we just need to stay vigilant . and keep doing the work until more information becomes apparent, hopefully, I am wrong. Hopefully, they walk into the dig site after a long bout with food poisoning."

Nadene nodded her headed and tried to shift gears to the research and the dig site developments but couldn't quite get the tone of worry out of her voice.

***

The drive through the traffic was to be expected, not a lot of conversation during, but once the directions were given through the GPS, developments were discussed. New technology was being used to investigate some of the narrow shaft the team had discovered two days ago. It was a combination of photography and history in an A.I. system that would extrapolate to create a full picture that the team could use as a map. This could only be done though with time, as this area had little conventionally recorded information. The site was trying to rebuild the foundations of the original Library of Alexandria.

Very little historical data, outside of what remained of blueprints from the era were available, was available even in academia. The current Library was supposedly built on top of the ruins, but their theory believed that there was an older Library of Alexandria. Those were the foundations they were looking for. The idea that the foundations were deeper and there was a whole other area of the library underground was still a new and ground-breaking theory. But this was the joint theory of Dr. Nadene and Dr. Alexandria with the Museum of Antiquity of Egypt. This had been the idea behind their research for years. Something about the remains of the blueprints never made sense, there was space unaccounted for.

Chapter XIV

The A.I. unit was a small compact camera that was attached to what was basically a very long slender pole. This pole was used as a guide into places that were either too delicate to get too or had no obvious opening. Both were the case here. The team had found a few false openings but had yet to find an opening into the main chamber beneath the floors of the ancient library. That changed yesterday when Dr. Jansen was brushing away at a space that was theoretically in the center of the library remains, when she found it. It was a tiny brass piece no larger than a button that said "αγορα". The brass piece was very carefully removed, to discover just earth beneath. Something about the placement felt so odd, like there was more to it. They drilled a small hole or attempted to: the floor was such a hard material that the drilling was very slow. The team finally broke through, just as Dr. Jansen arrived with Alena and Alexandria Martin.

"Dr. Nadene! We made it! We are through!" a young male assistant cried, when he saw the anthropologist exit the vehicle.

"That's fantastic!" Dr. Nadene's short blonde hair blew about her face in the wind, "Please, David, assist our new recruits!" The wind had picked up quite a bit since Alena and Alexandria had left the airport. The team was scrambling as quickly as possible to cover what they could of the dig site with weighted tarps.

There were a couple tents or tent like structures within the site, one Alena knew for certainty one for any documents, and the other for fragments, and any other research that would be organized and recorded. This was the larger of the four tents, as the other two were more exposed, portable, and likely the tents that were used on a daily basis as to where the team was digging for that day. Everyone headed into the larger of the tents, carefully moving the tables out of the way. The wind was settling down after a few minutes in the tent and came to a still after a few more moments.

The team went back to the tent that was central to the dig. The drill was still under the tent, having barely moved due to its weight. A small hole near it was just large enough for the A.I. camera to easily go through. Very carefully, Dr. Nadene connected the pieces of the A.I as Dr.

Alexandria connected a camera to the other end so as to act as a distant monitor. There was not a sound as the A.I. camera unit was guided down into the unknown room below their feet.

A couple feet down there was an open chamber. It was huge. Something lined the walls, but it was hard to tell as the distance was significant. There was some kind of opening in the walls. The image was not clear as there was no light. Not a sound went through the team, it was almost as though everyone was holding their breath. The tension was palpable. All their research and years of hunting had finally come to a head, they hoped. Ever so slowly the tiny camera on the end was turned, in a meticulous way, to get as full a panorama view as possible.

Nearing the end of the circumference Alexandria Martin gasped, breaking the silence that even the sands had not disturbed "Stairs."

She had said it so quietly that only Alena, who was crouched right next to her, had heard her say it. Alena very gently grabbed the monitor, and slowly turned the A.I. back to the spot. Through the darkness and dust of the ancient sands she could see the faint outline of stairs.

"Oh my—" Alena whispered.

"Let me see," Nadene grabbed it from Alena gently but with haste.

There was a slow rise in the group, chatter began as to where they could be, as the darkness made it difficult to see for certain.

"None of the tools, picked up on these," Nadene stated in puzzlement, "how-- I don't understand. It must be made of the identical material."

"It would have to be, but it still doesn't make since why they wouldn't register," Said Alexandria.

"What kind of material is this?" Alena chimed in, crouching down to touch the floor.

"It's a combination of minerals." replied the male named David.

"Like a Granite composition? Some granites have been known to have magnetic properties." She lifted her fingers, after moving sand around to feel the granite, still oddly smooth after centuries beneath the sands of Egypt.

"That might explain why we couldn't get a visual, it sends a pulse but it's not always accurate due to electromagnetic interference. I wonder how long it would take to get down there." Nadene said.

"Well, it looks like," Alexandria started and paused carefully grabbing and twisting the camera back towards the stairs. "If we can see them in this light then they must be somewhere close, maybe underneath." She said as she zoomed in with the camera on the monitor.

Alena, still carefully crouched on the ground in the sun, had an idea. She pulled the small brush out of her back pocket and began slowly clearing the sands away from the granite. The majority of the layers had already been cleared, but she was looking for a detail. Alena was not sure what the detail would be, but she would know it when she saw it, her gut clenched as she continued to swipe. Slowly but surely, she reached the granite and had cleared a space about two feet by two feet but still nothing. At this point everyone had taken notice, but no one questioned or stopped her. They were captivated in an attempt to figure out what she was doing.

Alena suddenly stopped. She put the brush down slowly and blew very carefully, that's when Alexandria and Nadene saw it. A thin line in the earth appeared. It was deep, penetrating through the sand, cutting into the granite. It was deeper than a typical crack between flooring. This space was dark, and without any trace of grout to keep the slabs of granite together. Alena followed the straight crack, a beautifully clean cut in the heavy rock. It stopped a couple inches up and came into a sharp edge—the corner. She carefully, hurriedly found the edges of the slab. It created a three foot by three-foot squared slab, a perfect metric yard. Though the granite was beautifully marbled and speckled with color, Alena noticed something interesting. On one side of the slab on edge was ever-so-slightly worn, making the edge softer. Alena touched the granite, again it was so smooth after centuries beneath the sand. She tried to move it and to her surprise there was little resistance.

"I wonder" Alena whispered to herself.

"What are you thinking, I see those wheels spinning." Alexandria eyed her daughter trying to make the connection herself.

Alena kneeled down and ran her hand over the worn spot. This is crazy, she thought as she tried to lift the piece of granite. Everyone leaned in to try and catch her but stopped short with protest when the slab actually lifted.

The slab had been hollowed out in a clean square, with a narrow ledge to hold it up, with fragments of rope still attached. It was a door to the stairway they had just discovered. They had found the way in. There was a lip that surrounded the edges with just enough space for the slab to stay in place and have space to walk down the narrow stairs.

"Who wants to go down the to the creepy chamber, first?" one of the interns had said.

Alena smiled. She knew that Nadene, Alexandria and herself would be going first, as the three of them had the most experience out of the team. But before they could go anywhere, they stopped and documented what they had just found. One of the interns grabbed the camera and started taking a few quick snapshots of everything. While the interns and less experienced anthropology students were writing and documenting inventory on the slab Alexandria grabbed a few flashlights for their trip down while Nadene and Alena grabbed some of the other supplies, tiny chisels and hammers and baggies for samples as well as a few pairs of sanitary gloves. No one had been down here in centuries, they wanted to keep the site as untouched as possible for as long as possible.

The women reset and calibrated one of the three cameras, not including the A.I. unit, for the dark interior space and grabbed a couple of refills of water. Unsure of the weight or how they were built the women went one-by-one, carefully down the stone steps. Once back on solid ground, Alena paused to let her eyes adjust to the darkness. It wasn't really that dark but greyer as she could see what was there but nothing really defined or clear was visible unless close-up. Alexandria pulled out her flashlight. Alena grabbed her recorder that she always carried on her. Although words never did the sight justice, it would certainly help when they document things. She did the same thing when she went to a crime scene.

Alena whispered and began to quietly describe the room, while Nadene and Alexandria slowly illuminated the walls and contents. The room was large and spacious. It was also a bit chilled and stuffy. She forgot that she was underneath a searing sun and was reminded of an old archival library she had once visited before she turned the flashlights on. Alena moved forward, now turning on her flashlight. Right in front of her was a wall to the chamber with a doorway that led to another room and another doorway. Each of the four walls did this. There were three additional chambers to each wall all with open doorways. Nadene walked back to the center of the largest chamber, the one they had just entered.

"Okay so how do you want to do this?"

"I noticed there are what appear to be clay oil lamps, a couple on the floor but also a couple of torches on each wall." Alexandria said in very excited tone.

"I saw those too. It's strange, the layout of this space is so open and then the additional rooms, but there is a closed door or different colored wall on the North West. There is a slight pigmentation to it. I think I saw some writing on it. I saw it after I walked a bit into the first chamber and flashed through the shelving."

"What is this place?" Nadene asked.

"Does anybody have a light, so we can find out?" Alexandria offered.

Alena smiled, "You know I don't leave home without it."

Nadene and Alexandria chuckled as Alena reached into her small bag that she had packed with a little bit of supplies and pulled out a zippo lighter. Each woman grabbed a small oil lamp and Alena lit each one and a couple of the torches. Light flooded the room, suddenly making it feel less dank and old. The cobwebs started to burn around the torches and added to the light. They moved together into each room starting with the eastern most room and lit a torch in each chamber. Now, they could see that each room was made of a different stone type or color. The main room was the same colorful granite as the doorway slab, the first western chamber was made of a sandstone and quartz combination that seemed to sparkle with light came near it. While the last two chambers in the west were a smooth limestone that still had pigmentation and images on the walls. Alexandria nearly dropped her torch when she saw the images. It was so rare to find images let alone ones with the color nearly completely intact.

Each chamber had a couple of tables, long and ancient but strangely beautiful. The color of the wood still shone after all these years and had little ware to them. The tables were equipped with chairs of the same wood, a couple of clay oil lamps, and tiny ink wells of white alabaster. The women looked at each other. These artifacts were incredible, it was rare to find any of these items intact let alone multiples of them. Scrolls upon scrolls were carefully tucked away on the shelves that lined the walls.

"We found it" Nadene breathlessly whispered.

"The lost library of Alexandria" Alena finished her thought, "The *Archives* of the library"

"They must have been making copies of the scrolls, this is unbelievable" Alexandria was so quiet with her words that they barely heard her.

They walked through the other chambers and each room confirmed their idea that they had found the archives. Thousands of scrolls were carefully organized into these vast chambers of shelves. Now that the largest chamber was lit the women could see it was even bigger, because what they initially thought was a wall holding a torch was in fact a large pillar of support that then worked into the hallway and housed even more scrolls than they saw.

"This will take years to catalogue" Alexandria whispered.

"I know, isn't it great!" Nadene's excitement made her voice just above a whisper. "I will retire while they are still finding lost works from here." The women worked their way through the North chambers and then the Western room. It wasn't true west but more of a North-West. These rooms felt a little different. The chambers were not made of the limestone or sandstone and quartz but blocks of gilded black and white marble were placed about head-high and were a yard thick. This started with the second chamber. The first was like the other in the sandstone and quartz as the walls but there was another mineral that was scattered through the chamber. It was a rich and vivid blue. Possibly Lapis Lazuli, thought Alena as she made mental note of it. There was a small set of stairs that went into this first chamber allowing it to grow in size. This room had more scrolls and was filled to the near top of the room. A decrepit ladder, intact but very shaky, was being held up by the corner of the room. The shelves started after two smaller tables. But there were rows of the ancient shelves. They placed their torches in nearby holders and turned their flashlights on.

They carefully walked through the shelves in a single file, even though there was enough space for them to walk two-by-two. Every scroll on the shelves was a different size and style. Some were open and papyrus, but most were parchment with a dowel to support the document. The whole place had been untouched since the granite slab was placed over the stairs for the last time.

151

They barely breathed the stale air for fear that the whole place would vanish with one wrong breath. They crossed the breadth of the vast room and came upon a strange and huge slab. It looked as though it was large door, upon further inspection.

Alena turned to her left trying to explore the rest of the room. To the left there was a huge opening in the wall. The darkness only allowed them to see so much but Alena could see there was something in there.

"What is it?" Alexandria had only noticed that Alena was in the doorway of the opening. She was getting ready to show her the symbols on the door, but when she had looked back, Alena wasn't there. Alexandria and Nadene followed suit and pointed their flashlights to doorway. The room was small but deep. There were two torches on the doorway. Alena pulled the lighter out and lighted them. The light was enough to see the walls. It was a tomb.

There were openings in the walls big enough to store a body. Bones of what once were bodies lied in the openings, tiny shreds of fabric were still wrapped around the body. At the center, there was a gold and black marble pillar. Atop the pillar was an urn. A small plaque with an ancient Greek dialect was placed next to the urn.

"Mom, can you translate? I think it's a name." Alena said.

"Give me a second."

Alexandria Martin put her reading glasses on and looked through the bifocals. After taking a moment, Dr. Martin subconsciously dropped her jaw.

"What's it say?" Nadene Jansen broke the silence.

"It says," Alexandria breathed out a sigh, "It says "The First Female Librarian, Hypatia, teacher to all.""

Chapter XV

A ll the air seemed to be sucked out of the stale room at those words. They had found her. They had actually found Hypatia. She was stoned by a mob of Christians in 450 A.D. for being not only a Pagan but an educated Pagan. Alena placed her hand on the marble but felt something strange. There was a piece of wood sticking out of the marble.

"I think there is a scroll here."

"In the marble?"

"Yes," Alena pulled the scroll out, as gently as she could.

"Here, I have a feeling its not written in English."

Alexandria opened the scroll and tried to read it.

"This is going to take some work but what I can see and read is fragmentary."

"Try to piece it together."

"Okay, well, Hypatia…stoned…a student protected her. Her neck was severed to end pain. Umm… body burned and buried. That's all I can make out, it's enough to safely say that her body wasn't lost like many scholars believed."

"I cant believe we found her."

"I take it back, I don't think I will be able to retire." Nadene said with a smile on here lips.

"We don't have the tools to deal with it properly, but we can go examine the stone door."

"Right." Alena followed the other two women back to the door.

A smile came across Alena's lips, she couldn't help but wonder what they would find. She looked carefully at the stone that made up this door. She recognized it—it was significant, but she couldn't quiet recall the name. Alena felt the rock, it was smooth, but it wasn't quiet as smooth as the granite. Nadene's flashlight caught her attention.

"Nadene, do that again"

"What? This?" as she slowly moved her light across the rock again.

"Oh my god…its purple." Alena's hushed voice stopped everything.

"But that's not possible," Alexandria nearly stuttered the words out.

"Porphyry" Alena stated, "it's porphyry marble, something important is behind this."

"Porphyry wasn't even discovered until 18 AD, what is it doing in the archives. It would have only been mined a few years before the top was thought to be destroyed." Nadene looked at the door quizzically as she said this.

"I am not sure what it's doing here, but the fact is— It *is* here. Porphyry of this grade was only ever used for exceptionally important things like royal tombs or the busts of Roman tyrants. It was and remains very rare and expensive. I don't even want to fathom what this door would have cost." Alena said raising her tone just barely with sheer awe.

"Having just found a person who shouldn't be here either, according to traditional timelines, I am not sure what will find. I might even start to believe dragons exist."

"This door, no matter what it's made of isn't going to move easily," Alexandria said from the side of the door, a bit breathless. While Nadene and Alena had been admiring the stone, Alexandria was testing the weight, the best way she could in the moment—she pushed. It did not budge.

"Alex, you didn't seriously just try to move this?"

"What? I just wanted to see if it was like the slab, it wasn't," Alexandria said as she walked back towards them rubbing her shoulder.

"How on earth are we going to get in there without breaking the door?" Nadene asked no one in particular, as she stared at the rare purplish marble.

Alena was staring at it, this grandiose door. Wanting so badly to just break it down and see what's behind, while at the same time not wanting to touch the door without the utmost care. Alexandria and Nadene were looking at it with Alena, when Nadene gasped.

"What is it?"

"There are patterns, I am seeing patterns, look— LOOK!" Nadene's voice was almost to normal volume levels.

"You're right, why does that look familiar—oh my!"

"Mom, what is it?"

"It's writing," she was looking intently at the top and slowly worked her way down, her breath caught in realization "There's pieces of Sumerian mixed with the Greek! That's not possible!"

Chapter XVI

I have your responsibilities. MR and KM are cherished by many and admired in their fields. It would be a shame for them to perish in the purple sands of time among their dreams and work of parchment. If you don't find them, they will suffocate like the scrolls of antiquity. In a place only just revealed. Not much time before I strike again. Tick Tock...

A keeper

Perfect. The young man put down the pen that will set the rest of the plan and the trap in motion. This was the precursor moment that had been planned for months now. Finally, he would confront a problem he had never had the opportunity to deal with, but he will soon see her. His methodology may not be exactly up to code with the organization that he had just recently been accepted into, but each problem has a unique solution. He was going to get two bird with one stone on this mission, stop the women in charge of this grasp for knowledge that was hidden for so long and destroy the woman who destroyed his life by never being there for him. Yet she was always there for another. Before he was through with her and the mission, more than one person would have suffered for this loss.

He quietly unlocked the door to Dr. Nadene Jansen's room and carefully placed the note on her tiny table near the door. She was already in bed asleep. He crept back in near silence to the door, but the floorboard, inches away creaked. He moved swiftly, not even looking if she had heard, out the door. Standing for just a moment long enough to hear if she moved. She didn't. Carefully he walked down the stairs and paused at the room shared by Dr. Martin and her daughter. He couldn't resist. He picked the lock ever so quietly and looked in for just a moment. Both women were sound asleep, Dr. Martin was the smart one. She was facing towards the door. *She is so peaceful, her world will shortly shatter,* he thought.

He had only recently found out who his mother was, thanks to father keeping track of him all these years. He had kept records of everything. She had given him up almost immediately after his birth, she didn't want him. Yet, only a couple years later, according to his father's record she got married and had a child with this man. She had changed her name, but his father knew who she was. He had given him everything he had ever needed as proof against her. *She didn't want me…*

Chapter XVII

James Benakis stood staring at the garden just outside his office window. He liked working in the earth, there was something so calming about getting dirt beneath one's fingers. James like to garden and work in the earth, growing up he had often spent time with the estate gardener. The gardens sprawled out over what land remained on the estate. Over the generations, land was bought, sold, resold and later donated. Some even went to a local cricket club just down the road. The house foundations date back to the mid- 17th century but the interior structure was an exquisite blend of Victorian slendor with a replicated Tudor exterior. Its unique beauty rivaled even the royal palaces. The gardens were added in the early 18th century by Sir Robert Browne Wiles. This was the ancestor of James Benakis. Sir Wiles's family had purchased the land and the ruins of the home in the late 17th century. Sir Robert Wiles's hobby was floristry and gardening, making a garden for the estate a clear addition. The gardens were immaculate ever since. The house, in both World Wars served as an Mi6 codebreaker headquarters. It was one of a few that had been utilized. James Benakis couldn't help but think of the rich history of his home when he looked at the golden-stoned parapets, stained glass in the dining room or even the orange rose-filled gardens. This place was a wonder to behold, living, breathing history is what he woke up in every day. The staircase was a bit of pain as he had gotten longer in his years but he wouldn't change priceless piece of artwork by adding a stairlift. He refused to change anything unless absolutely necessary. James remember the anguish he and Blanche had gone through when they put the house through renovations. It needed to be done but every little decision he insisted on signing off and knowing the reason behind the architect's decision.

The estate was of great size, he had only realized this in his old age. The house had several rooms, the upper and lower levels connected by an impressive and hand-crafted staircase. The artwork that hung on the beautiful walls made the home even more impressive than it was without it. These were original works from the renaissance through modern artwork and each room had a number of pieces that were themed to the room. Many landscapes from around the world, so that the house almost felt as though it had windows throughout time and space.

He loved this place. His family had been known for their philanthropic tradition of donating to the arts and education for all. Sometimes, the family was compensated with the artwork or purchased it at charity auctions and bought above requested, donating the difference. He continued this, often times in his sisters' names.

James Benakis had walked through the double French doors, gardening tools in hand when his phone rang. It was the young detective he had put on his assignment. He hadn't thought he would hear from her for some time, knowing how vague the information was that he gave her is. But her phone call wasn't in fact about the case but just simply a courtesy call.

"Hello?" James said when he swiped the answer button to answer the phone.

"Mr. Benakis?" The young woman questioned, "This is Detective Alena Martin, I apologize I am calling to tell you something has come up and I won't be able to work on your case as often as I would have liked but I have read the files. It appears to me that your sister may have run away from something. There was never a body found. In that day, records were a bit easier to falsify, so she may have run away, changed identities and moved on. Cutting everyone out of her life who knew her up to that point. However, the motivation is what I am working on and I will let you know if I come up with any clues or anything. I just didn't want you to think I had forgotten."

James didn't interrupt her until she paused long enough to feel like she had finished, "I understand and appreciate your diligence. If I think of anything further, I will let you know but at this moment I can't recall. Maybe we can talk in another couple weeks and see if anything else comes to mind or whenever you may have time?"

"Sure, Mr. Benakis that would be fine."

"Great, goodbye for now."

"Good bye"

He hung up the phone, knowing he didn't have a lot of time left in this world, however, he did have enough time to wait on this. He stared out on his family's estate that he had inherited. He liked to have at least one day a week to himself with the quiet sounds of the garden. Some days it was so quiet that he could still hear the sound of the flowers growing and the bees buzzing across the flowers. His favorite time was to go out into the garden after a hard rain. The smell of the dirt changed, warm and damp, it became the smell of petrichor. The flowers' scent would waft through the windows like a siren's call the next morning.

The Benakis estate was removed from the city but was just a short drive to it. He lived just outside of London, but preferred physical proximity to the city while also staying removed.

James Benakis gathered what few tools he used to garden and walked through the house, after kicking off his shoes at the door. He went to his office with his tools, being careful not to get dirt on the ornate rugs. He placed them by the fire place of his small study. He had thought of something while he was gardening. There was something he hadn't told the young detective. But he wanted to confirm his thoughts. He opened his family pictures scrapbook that his wife had made years before she had passed away. He flipped to the family photos, he was looking for one that had his oldest sister in it. He saw it, the man standing next to her, the man she was engaged to before she disappeared.

There had always been something about this William Pritcherson that he had never liked but had never been able to place. William had always read like he was hiding something. He never read as much of a family man, more of a power-hungry narcissist. James put the book down and wrote his name down and had the phone in his hand when he felt a pain in his left arm. Instead of calling the detective, he dialed 112 in hopes that the paramedics would come soon.

Chapter XVIII

The walkie-talkie crackled to life with static. The sun was still beating down, but the heat had slowly died as the horizon turned a glowing orange and the green earth seemed to light up like flames. With Kendra Michelle and Sita missing Joey was now in charge of some of the supervision. Joey Blake was another intern but a graduate with a degree in engineering. He loved the culture of the Greeks and the history of the area. They were the first engineers. He had found a different perspective in his elective undergraduate anthropology course. So much so that every elective he could he took an anthropology class.

Joey Blake even designed some experimental tools for the field of archaeology for his Master's degree. One being a tool they had for this dig. It was designed to lift or open huge slabs of stone with ease and little pressure. The idea was to be able to move massive stones with writing on

them without heavy lifting. He called it the S.E.S.A.M.E
(Safe Execution of Sealed Archives with Massive cuneus
Extractor).

Joey grabbed the walkie and pushed his thick
lensed, turtle-shell rimmed glasses back onto the bridge of
his nose. "Can you repeat?"

Static cleared out a bit as he heard "We need a team
down here. We found something…something big" it was
Dr. Jansen's voice.

"Doctor, it's getting dark up here. We are running
out of daylight."

"Good to know, we are coming up, we will regroup
and comeback down with a plan tomorrow. Do you think
we can set up the simple rig to open something…like a
door?" she said it with such excitement that Joey said
probably.

Joey grabbed his team together. It was mix of
people he knew were experienced with the S.E.S.A.M.E.
and a couple of heavy lifting volunteers and a graduate
archaeology student. He then left a charged walkie-talkie
with one of the other graduate students and headed
carefully down with the team and the equipment. There
were only three walkie-talkies, he remembered to grab his,
assuming that the first one might be low on battery.

Though the chamber was mostly dark there was some light thanks to the torches. Once he and the team were all in the main chamber with the equipment, he got back on the walkie, "Where are you?"

"Joey, we are in the Northern chamber and the furthest chamber in that grouping."

Joey turned to the North and was stunned by the sheer size of everything. His eyes had adjusted to the limited light and leaded the group to the rooms. He wanted to stop every few feet to see the scrolls and to touch them just to ensure they were real, but he didn't. Nothing in the world compared to the feeling of discovering something no one had seen in centuries. His parents had wanted him to go to medical school like they had. His father was a radiologist and his mother was a surgeon. Joey never even tried to go into medical school, his brother filled that void. Keith Blake was Joey's younger brother and he was studying medical law. Joey went into experimental engineering. His advisor had read his thesis and passed it along to Dr. Jansen, that was the first step on his journey to where he stood now. In a room hundreds of years old and in near pristine condition. There was a little bit of sand and earth on the stone, but the temperature was just right from preservation. The wood was a little delicate though this hardly surprised Joey.

He carefully walked through the shelves, "Don't touch anything, we don't have the proper equipment and we don't want to damage anything," Joey reminded everyone as well as an out loud reminder for himself.

They reached the spot where the doctor was with Dr. Martin and Alena. But he stopped short in step and breath. The size of the purple marble door was bigger than he expected and far more beautiful in details. Joey didn't think that they had anything big enough to prop that door open, but an engineering was nothing if not resourceful.

"My God…" the words slipped out of Joey's mouth.

"Yes, we know."

"We are losing sunlight," Joey said, once he regained his composure.

"Yes, we know that too, the temperature started to drop a few minutes ago." Dr. Martin said.

"We had an idea on how to open this, there are some kind of hinges on this of the door, but not the other." Alena Martin had said. Joey had only seen the knowledgeable beauty from a far. But now that she was right in front of him, she seemed very approachable.

"Okay, what's the idea."

Alena told him that if they set up the S.E.S.A.M.E equipment that typically opens smaller doors and lifts lids it might still work. The door didn't seem to be as heavy as it looked. They had found a small hole that looked deliberately created and it gave them an idea that maybe parts of it had been hollowed out.

"If we leave the equipment here and set it up like, you normally would. Maybe leave it on for a couple of hours or overnight it might be open by the morning."

The S.E.S.A.M.E was really nothing more than a glorified, electric wedge crowbar system that had been rigged together. The door was ten feet tall and a solid slab without the appearance of any cracks, they wanted to keep it that way. The team had grabbed the ladder and was now propping it up against the wall. The rig in theory extended about twelve feet tall give or take the safety measures implemented. It moved slowly on an extremely long bike chain attached to a small motor as it wedged into the space, lifting the slab slowly and hopefully without cracks. A mallet, operated by the motor and computer, would tap the massive hand-crafted carbon-fiber wedges at one-foot intervals, that were both lightweight but strong to do the heavy lifting into the gap between the door and wall. The whole unit would move up so as to avoid too much pressure in one spot. The wedges were roughly three feet at the widest point, enough space to get a couple people through the door. Joey had created add-ons and different tools for this equipment and was excited to use his thesis in practice. In this case, things were going to get interesting, he hadn't used it on a marble door.

The tool was computerized and could be left alone, but they were going to do it in shifts. The mallet started at the top and carefully worked its way down the wedges and up the door until the door was open to about three feet. The tool was drilled into the earth and had industrial grade suction cups attached to the legs. When it was all setup in looked like one-half of a giant centipede crawling up the wall.

The computer monitor was simple and there was a keyboard attached. The four keys that were worn the most, 'start', 'stop', 'wait' and 'on'. The 'start' and 'on' buttons are the obvious meaning, the 'stop' would shut down the entire system, and 'wait' would stop the equipment but not the computer. Joey breathed a nervous exhale. He was finally putting the work and research to the test after countless trials and errors. Joey kneeled down to the small hovering monitor and keyboard.

He sucked in some air as he pressed the 'on' key. It started to make a slight buzzing noise, the small engine-like generator being the source. Nothing sounded out of the ordinary. Joey put some numbers into the open code form that flashed onto the monitor. The small monitor showed some numbers then a symbol of buffering was circling. It was working. It was actually working; the sensors were gathering the height and estimated the weight of the door. An estimated time of twelve hours with a gentle force against the posts to open the door.

"Twelve hours. Okay, we will do this in shifts."

"We should do the first six hours, Dr. Jansen, my team and I know this machine and if something goes wrong, we will be here, you three should go get some rest. We will take it in shifts here too." Joey stated so mater-of-factly that Dr. Jansen didn't argue.

"Thank you, Joey" Alena said, she shook hands with Joey and walked back out of the chambers with Dr. Martin and Dr. Jansen following.

"Oh Joey—"

"If I find anything, you're the first one I call, I know, please go get some rest."

Dr. Jansen smiled and turned. Once the three women were out of ear shot, Joey and his team put on their protective headphones as Joey hit the 'start' button. There was a pause and then a loud hit on the first post. The mallet made more noise than the actual force on the wedges. This extra sound was due to the echoes off the walls. It wasn't too loud but there were just enough reverberations that protective headphones were a good idea.

The Secret

Chapter XIX

Peter walked into his real hotel room after having dinner in a local little shawarma shop. His room at the local little hotel with the dig team was for appearances but he avoids the area as much as possible. With his new-found family money, he decided to enjoy life a bit while here in Egypt. He had quietly booked a modest hotel room at one of the nicer hotels. It was clean and almost luxurious by comparison to the expedition's booked hotel. He laid out on the bed in the spacious bedroom and looked out the window at the view of the city of Alexandria.

A modern city by most means with stark contrasts of ruins still visible throughout the city. He undressed from his buttoned-down shirt, trousers in navy, and Italian leather slip-on shoes into an old t-shirt, ratty jeans, and an old pair of sneakers. He had some cleaning up of loose ends to deal with and some intimidation to instill. They had to stop looking, or they would find everything. Every "lost" article in the Library of Alexandria had never been lost but copied and placed in the sacred vault.

This vault had just been found. Alexandria Martin, Nadene Jansen and Alena Martin had found it. It was within their grasp. He was losing time. He was sliding on his sneakers when his cell-phone buzzed. He double-checked to ensure that it wasn't the private cell-phone that only the organization had to contact with. It wasn't. It was his regular number.

"Yes?"

"Hey, Peter, this is Joey from the dig, I was wondering if you would like to come check out something great! The door is slowly opening, and I was hoping you would take a couple hours watch before we call in the doctors?"

"Sure"

"Great, see you soon!"

***

A figure in a hotel room stood with a phone to his ear. The lights were off so that if anyone did look in, they couldn't see anything.

"Yes, tonight, I have to perfect place. The false keepers will be shaken, and the doctors blamed. This will end the dig site."

"Do you have a plan of placement and escape?" the voice urgently asked on the other line.

"Yes, I will place them and then drive back to my hotel room and book a flight."

"Make sure you leave before anyone finds out. I assume you left your signature note?"

"Already in place." Stated the figure in shadows.

The line clicked. This would be perfect. He would have the perfect stage to lay all his cards down in one play. It would be brutal and in theory a couple of people will lose their lives but only if time goes wrong. Peter wanted to avoid collateral damage, but things happen. He walked out of his main room and caught the elevator to the basement floor where his car was parked. The light banging on the trunk had started again. He clicked the button on his keyring to lift the trunk automatically.

The dark curls of hair covered the Caribbean woman's face, the other girl's face was turned away as though she didn't even want to see him. Their hands and ankles were tightly bound, but not too tight, with black zip ties, he didn't want to break flesh or burn it with duct tape. Mouths were gagged with a cloth and then that was taped to prevent movement. They had no choice, Kendra had managed to get out of her duct tape wrist binding, so he had to retie both with the zip ties to the wrists, but he couldn't do that with her awake.

He opened the car door and grabbed the couple of linen rags he kept, grabbed the chloroform that was safely tucked in a padded pouch beneath the driver's seat, and poured just a bit out on to the cloth. He went back to Kendra and managed to secure it against her nose even with the fight she put up. He repeated the action for Sita but with less of a fight, partly because she was smaller but also because she just didn't have a lot of fight left in her.

He put his supplies away and started the ignition for a quiet ride to the outskirts and the rare greenery of Egypt that the site was at. He would place them where they would be found but whether they will be alive when found depends on when the doctors see the note. Everything was going according to plan.

**

Beneath the hood of the trunk, just as they were slipping into another horrifically calm unconsciousness, Sita reached her hands for Kendra's. Kendra had slipped into the unconsciousness and the man had made sure she was out before he was sloppy and put the chloroform just beneath her nose as a reapplication. She had tried to tell Kendra to not struggle or fight, to wait until an opportunity arose to escape. But no opportunity had come in two days for Sita, prior to Kendra, and nothing had shown since. They hadn't had a clear look at his face until this exchange. She just felt the grip of Kendra's fingers as she realized she recognized the man's face and lost her fight to stay awake.

Chapter XX

Peter drove up to the dig site and killed the engine. He checked to make sure that the parking brake was up, then walked towards the tent. He grabbed a pair of gloves that were laying on a table and bumped into Joey on his way to the stairs.

"Oh, hey, Peter! That was fast!"

"I was in the area for dinner and got your call. How open is the door now?" Peter asked, never breaking his facade.

Joey pushed his glasses back up to the top of his bridge and heaved a post like piece of equipment to get a better grip. "It's about a foot and a half going on two feet, I was able to remove these posts to give it more space and less risk of these falling after the door is open to about thee feet."

"Great, is your team on its way out, now that it's all set up and working? I can watch it for a couple of hours, it ought to be a one-man job by now."

"Yea, no it is, I'll explain what to do if something does go wrong, but also just to keep an eye on it." Joey said as he walked towards the tent to put the posts in their protective case.

"Great."

Joey and Peter walked back down the ancient stairs and into the long, extraordinary rooms, towards a beating sound that got a bit louder with every step. Joey handed Peter a pair of headphones identical to the pair he was now wearing. They reached the source of the pounding. A huge rod with extensions attached to the wall and wedge-shaped posts in the middle of the rod attached by slender carbon-fiber support beams. These were all connected to the small hovering monitor and generator rooted at the bottom of the rod in the earth and granite. The footprint of this enormous piece of equipment was very small. The only damage was a small hole where the drill was anchored.

Joey crouched down to the monitor and tapped the screen. It flashed white and came to life. He double-tapped it and a pop-up came up "Do you wish to stop or wait?" he tapped the 'wait' key that was on the small keyboard attached to the monitor. The machine stopped mid-pound and slowly brought the mallet back to the rod support.

"Now, that this is paused," Joey stretched his jaw as though to relax his ears or maybe unclench the muscles of his face. "Ah, there, okay. So, this, once I start it back up will continue until the door is open, it has about another six hours left. I wasn't going to call in the docs until there was about two hours left."

"Sounds like a plan."

"Cool, see you soon." He replaced his headphones and pressed the start button.

About twenty minutes of pounding passed before Peter's secret phone buzzed with a text message *I am here, need assistance.*

***

They had dinner before they went up to their rooms and each swiftly fell asleep. They had set their alarms for about an eight hours sleep. Alena and Alexandria's alarms went off and each hit snooze, only to hear Nadene run across the hall and down the stairs moments after.

"Someone has been in my room! The girls are in danger!" She said breathlessly hovering at the door.

"I don't understand, what do you mean. Come in, out of the doorway." Alexandria said before Nadene could interrupt.

Alena noticed the piece of paper in Nadene's hand. It was slightly crumpled with her grip, but it was otherwise crisp. The writing was handwritten and clean though it may have been written in haste with the last word lightly smudged. After looking at the note, Alena actually read it. She drew in a sharp breath as she reread the note that had been placed on Nadene's table at the hotel.

"This was on my table when I woke up."

"This is what I was expecting, things just got worse."

"What do you mean?" Alexandria finally looked up at Alena after getting water for Nadene to calm down.

"It's a ransom note, kind of, it's more of a threat."

"I had hoped that the girls had only lost track of time or something I never dreamed they were actually kidnapped."

"Alena, what's it say?"

"It's a riddle," Alena said without answering the question, "It's a riddle to where they are being held."

Alena walked to the tiny table between the two beds in the room. "Mom—" before Alena could finish the thought Alexandria was already in her daughter's bag looking for a pen and paper. "Thanks," Alena smiled when Alexandria put the highlighter and paper on the table. She began highlighting key phrases in the small lines of text, then wrote them on the spare sheet of paper. Alena was trying to make some kind of connection to the words. She knew they were meant to see it otherwise it wouldn't have been left in plain sight. The wording of certain phrases is what caught her attention. She was mildly impressed with this person's ability to pack so much into so little a space.

I have your responsibilities. MR and KM are cherished by many and admired in their fields. It would be a shame for them to perish in the purple sands of time among their dreams and work of parchment. If you don't find them, they will suffocate like the scrolls of antiquity. In a place only just revealed. Not much time before I strike again. Tick Tock...
A keeper

On the paper Alena connected the key phrases that were out of place...MR and KM...in their fields...purple sands...suffocate...just revealed...strike again. She looked up and realized she knew where they were.

"He's trying to detach himself from what he's about to do, that's why they are referenced by their initials and your responsibilities." She explained, "They were taken here when they were headed to the field of work. 'Purple sands' that phrase has something important, maybe among the royalty?" Alena paused from thinking aloud and mulled it over. "No only just revealed and purple sands are connected. He knows about the door. 'Suffocate...'" Alena paused again, unsure. Then it hit her like a ton of bricks.

"Oh my god…they're in the room behind the porphyry marble," Alena stated in such a hushed tone that it seemed as though all the air had been sucked out with the revelation. After a beat, "We have to go back. He's going to kill them. The parchment, it takes a long time for it to suffocate and dry out, that's the clue. We don't have a lot of time."

"I have the keys." Nadene headed towards the door. Alexandria and Alena were just behind her to close the door. They ran down the couple flights of stairs to the car.

Once they started the car, Alexandria dialed up her phone in an attempt to call Joey but instead of an answer the voicemail received their call. She hung up. "Who was supposed to take over after Joey's team? Who was next on shift?"

"I don't know, we didn't discuss it. I just assumed that the boys would take shifts." Nadene said slowly, realizing her mistake.

"We might be on our own on this." Alena said aloud.

A sense of dread filled the car. Not knowing what they would find put the women on edge for the duration of the ride. They arrived but no sign of anyone was present at the dig site. No vehicle, which generally meant no one was here.

"Something's not right." Alena said as she pulled out her personal weapon, a Glock 19 with a differentiated handle so as not to confuse it with her work weapon.

"You didn't tell me you brought that?" Alexandria said a bit alarmed.

"Just following instincts, foreign country, not the friendliest to women, and I am trained to use it." Alena shrugged as though it was no big deal. For her if the force taught her one thing, it was to always be prepared. Alena was putting in a magazine into the weapon as they walked through the tents to the stairs in the earth.

"I don't like it either, but can you at least holster it?" Nadene asked.

"Sure, I was just getting ready to" as she grabbed her leather shoulder holster. Alena wrapped it over her left shoulder, being right-handed that had always been the more comfortable placement.

"How did you remember to grab this when I forgot my phone, speaking of, does someone have a phone?" Asked Dr. Jansen, a bit annoyed with her forgetful self. Nadene had quickly tossed on a cream blouse and her cargo kakis before leaving but hadn't tucked in her shirt, in order to prevent sand from creeping in with the wind.

"Yep, let's go" Alena said as she shifted her basic blue buttoned shirt underneath the holster, placing her gun in it. Grateful that she was wearing her denim jeans, in the chill of the early morning.

"Be my guest," Nadene said. As the breeze picked-up, all three tucked in their shirts before leaving the car. Alexandria followed Alena after putting her phone in her pocket of her dark denim jeans. Alexandria had sewn on a buttoned top to secure the phone, months ago, because she always had the problem of her phone slipping or shifting. Nadene stopped inside the tent and grabbed a light for each of them and followed behind.

As they neared the stairs, they stopped dead in their tracks. There wasn't a sound. The machine to open the door had been stopped. Alexandria checked her watch, "That can't be right, it should have another several hours."

Not knowing how long it had been stopped or if it had been stopped by something other than the keys for the monitor, they stayed there for a moment longer listening for anything else. When nothing was heard, they turned on their flashlights. With light illuminating the stairs they carefully went down together, wanting to stay close in the dark. They stood at the bottom and slowly turned, backs to each other, and lighted every bit to ensure no one was here.

They moved to the chamber with the door as the lights were still there. The torches were still burning, which was surprising, but they were dim in the dark. Joey had propped up a huge light to illuminate the machine and insure that he could see it. The pounding of the mallet wasn't present but even in this dim light Alena could see that the door was open about a couple feet. They walked quietly on the stone floor. Every few yards they would stop, until they reached the last chamber. It contained the most scrolls and shelves, if anybody was hiding Alena thought it would be here. She would stop and listen, but it was hard to hear anything beyond her own heart pounding. She could hear the soft controlled breathing of her mother and Nadene, but otherwise nothing. If someone is here, she couldn't tell, which was of little comfort. They reached the door to see that it was open at least two and a half feet wide, plenty of space for someone to walk through.

"I'll go first and let you know if it's clear," Alena said, "after all, I am the one who is armed."

"Be careful," Alexandria said, more nervous than she would ever admit.

"I'll move the light to the opening, that should give you a bit of better coverage than the handheld." Nadene stated as she headed for the light.

"Thanks, Nada," Alena said remembering her years growing up with Nadene around for much of it. She was more family than friend at this point in her life.

TEA TIME

"Be right back," Alena said as she pulled out her gun and turned the safety off. She looked to her mother and walked through the door.

Chapter XXI

"Mr. Benakis?" a young woman in scrubs gently nudged the older gentleman in the hospital bed. He was now under her care. He had been brought in just a few hours ago with a cardiac arrest. She was one of three doctor on duty. Dr. Greene she had to go into surgery a few minutes after he showed up for a child. She left Mr. Benakis in the very skilled care of her nurses when she had to scrub in. Gratefully, both had made it. But now that she had a minute, she wanted to check on Mr. Benakis.

"Sir?" she prompted again. Her nurses had been checking on him but said he would be awake for a couple minutes and then go back under. They needed a contact, if he had anybody. He started to come around slowly. His eyes fluttered and then opened fully.

"Sir, I'm Dr. Greene. Sir, do you know where you are?" the woman asked.

"I'm guessing by the sterile colors and smell, my lawyer's office?" he said rather groggily. He tried to make the words sound light, but he wasn't fully awake. "Aye kid, I'm in the hospital correct?"

"Yes, do you remember how you got here?" she smiled mildly amused glad that he had a sense of humor.

"I had a heart attack." Now awake, "I remember pieces like calling the paramedics but then I think I blacked out." He said.

"Well, there is no other damage, so you didn't hit anything when you blacked out," she was looking at his chart and then looked up at him "but we are going to keep you a couple days just to make sure. Is there anybody we can call for you?" He was fit and in shape, so when she saw cancer patient on his chart, her surprise was hard to conceal but she did.

"Not at the moment but maybe later. I would just like to rest."

"That's fine, Mr. Benakis, let us know" She placed his chart back on his bed and by the time she reached the door, she could hear a light snore.

***

At that moment, several hundreds of miles away, the shadow of a man was standing as silently as he could behind a statue in the chamber behind the porphyry marble door. Then he saw lights. *Shit.* He wasn't supposed to be here. Now he had to change up a few things. He got as close to the edge of the statue as he dared to see if anyone was coming through.

A woman walked through, even with the limited lighting he could see that she was armed with a pistol. She thought that a firearm would be her protection when in fact the shadow man was not only armed himself, but he knew he could disarm her. He had the element of surprise. He hid again in the shadow of the statue and waited for her to pass. Carefully and with silence he moved to the darkness that the light couldn't reach, right next to the door. Never crossing the light for fear of casting a shadow and exposing himself. He stayed and waited in the corner. He watched her like a big cat watched their prey, with sheer focus.

She called "clear" and lifted her weapon as two other women walked in. They stood in the light and realized that there was something in front of them in darkness. Their handheld lights flickered on and he heard the slightest of gasps escape their lips.

He crouched, making himself even smaller, deeper into the shadows. All his years of training finally being put into play. Patience he thought, it takes one swift movement to the next step of the plan.

***

Alena walked through the door, gun in hand. She slowly passed the light to the corners and paused to listen, she didn't hear anything. She wasn't sure what she was expecting but it wasn't silence. *They are supposed to be here.* She did another sweep with her handheld light and saw something, it was a giant statue, nothing was moving so that was good for now. She turned her head towards the door, "Clear."

Nadene and Alexandria walked through the door one-by-one. Both of them turned on their handheld light, then slowly walked out of the small pool of light. That's when they saw it, behind the statue—drag marks, two sets. They rushed to the statue's shadow and sure enough two bodies were lying limp in shadow. The missing girls. Their wrists were zip-tied behind their backs, ankles zip-tied together and then to each other. Rope was wrapped several times in a body bind and knotted tightly. It looked like a wrapping that would only get tighter with a struggle. There was no way out for them without help. The most distressing item was a clear bag that was placed and taped over their faces. The girls were either asleep and very slowly suffocating or they had run out of time.

"Can you hear me, it's Dr. Nadene," Nadene said in utter distress, "does anybody have a sharp object? Oh wait--!" she stood up and reached into one of the lower cargo pockets pulled out her small folded pocket knife. Very carefully she cut a slit in the plastic of Sita's bag and handed the knife to Alexandria who was now kneeling next to Kendra. Alexandria repeated the action and closed the knife placing it next to her. Nadene stretched the slit into a big hole and Alexandria followed suit. Sita started to move as her body registered the influx of oxygenated air.

"Sita, don't move, it's Nadene, just breathe."

Kendra didn't move. Alena leaned down to check each girl's pulse and she could feel it. "They're alive, I think once the oxygen gets into their lungs, they will be okay, but we will have to take them to the hospital to determine for sure that there is no permanent damage, once we get them to the car." The bags were open, but Alena smelled something she recognized and suddenly felt woozy.

"Nadene, Mom, cover your face, it's chloroform." Alena put her sleeve in front of her face. The bags had been not only a death sentence for Kendra and Sita but a trap for them. Even if they got to the girls and got oxygen, the chloroform would have kept them here for a couple hours. Nadene caught the brunt of it as she was sitting in between the two girls. Alexandria stood up to try and distance herself.

"Kendra, can you hear me?" Nadene asked groggily. The chloroform was beginning to take hold.

"Nada, stand up," Alena said through her sleeve, "you have to get some distance."

Nadene fell straight into the small layer of sand over the earth that was part of the ancient stone floor. Alena and Alexandria's reflexes were compromised, and neither could catch her in time. Alena heard something—movement. Someone was in here with them. Alena spun but couldn't see anything but the statues. The drugs were blurring her vision with the temporary promise of sleep. She shook her head and turned back to her mom but saw someone behind her she fired her weapon twice but heard her bullets hit the statue behind him. She shook her head trying to loosen the grip of the chemical.

"Dammit!" Alena said, but when she re-aimed, he was gone, and her mother was out cold in the sand without a sound. She tried to spin but instead of spinning she felt a sharp pain on her back and then on the top of her head. She felt the cold sand against her face but never saw who hit

194

her. The last thing she saw was her gun being kicked out of in her hand.

***

Hours later, Nadene Jansen woke up to utter silence. She slowly sat up, shaking the fine-grained sand out of her short blonde hair. Slowly everything came rushing back. She noticed that the girls were slowly starting to move and wake. The knife she had used earlier was still folded next to Kendra. She reached over Kendra and grabbed it. Nadene, carefully but quickly, released the bonds of Kendra then Sita. Kendra was the first to fully wake up just as Nadene was lifting the bag off of her head then she reached over to Sita's a removed it. Sita woke a few minutes later.

Both women sat up slowly, with Nadene's assistance. Each woman slowly adjusted to what was going on as Nadene clued them in to where they were and what had happened. As she began telling them about how they had found them she realized something was missing. "Dr. Martin and Alena, her daughter, helped get you free and safe. Wait a second—" Nadene had been so concerned with getting Kendra and Sita safe that she hadn't noticed until now that Alexandria and Alena were missing.

TEA TIME

She stood up in hopes of seeing them just beyond the statue, *maybe the chloroform didn't hit them as hard, or they fell asleep just beyond.* That was when she saw them. The drag marks in the sandy areas leading to the door. There were two sets, one for each woman. There were two sets of foot prints where the drag marks suddenly stopped at the door. It figures she would get two colleagues back only to have the closest thing she had to family taken right from under her. Leading her to believe that Alex and Alena were the true targets, and this was all a trap to get to them. She stared in utter disbelief. "Do either of you—wait, never mind we will have to find a phone." Nadene said as she hid the rage beginning to build.

Chapter XXII

Alexandria groggily lifted her head, she tried to lift her hand to her forehead. She couldn't. She opened her eyes thinking is was a bad dream, but this foreign darkness would not lift. Immediately, she knew something was wrong. She gently shook her head. Alexandria could feel some kind of plastic restraint rubbing against her wristwatch. *Zip-ties.* She twisted her limbs, but she was definitely secured against the chair she was seated in. She breathed deeply, but for some reason that hurt.

She breathed as deeply as she could and held it to confirm her sudden suspicions. Yes, she was restrained across her ribs with what she figured was rope. Another security measure from this unknown assailant, she assumed. She shook her head to shake off the grogginess only to feel a sudden pain in the back of her head. It felt like a migraine but sharper and more focused, like she had been hit in the back of the head. Her memory was a little fuzzy. Dr. Martin couldn't remember anything after finding Sita and Kendra.

Then she remembered. Alexandria remembered everything when she thought about her daughter. She could feel her heart beating in her throat as she tried to call out. *Maybe she's here and I can't see her*, but nothing except a muffled scream came out. Her mouth was taped and gagged. That explained the ache that was in her jaw. She couldn't help but feel the fear in her chest as her heart continued to pound in her ears. She breathed and tried to control her breathing, slowing it with each breath. She didn't want whoever was out there to sense her fear. But Alexandria allowed herself to feel it, only then could she focus it and use it. The only thing she needed then was a target to use it on.

***

It was dark, not like a room but as though something was blocking her vision. Alena was groggy, like she had been drugged, but aware enough to know something was very wrong. Alena could feel the restrains against her wrists, her arms were tied to the chair. She could tell that she was seated and even her ankles were restrained, by some kind of plastic, zip-ties maybe, *at least it isn't duct tape*. She could sense her heart rate rising, she tried to breathe. She heard something: breathing—she wasn't alone. She tried to call out, but it was then that she realized she was being gagged. Through the muffled cry, she heard a different muffled cry that wasn't hers. The other person was here against their will as well.

She tried to move the gag with her tongue and shoulder, it wouldn't move. Alena tried to reach for it with her hand by moving her head closer, that was when she noticed the ropes around her ribs. She stopped when she felt pain. Anxiety began to course through her veins with a rush of fear. The last thing she remembered was finding the bodies of the assistants in the chamber. But that surely was a while ago, if the ache in her jaw, her head and ribs was any indication. Fear began to grip her, she tried to stay calm, but nothing really prepared her for this.

Footsteps. She could hear the soft tap of a pair of rubber soled shoes on tile. She breathed as level as she could as the steps got closer. She heard the other person's breathing elevate. The footsteps softened ever further when they came into contact with carpet, she could feel the vibrations in her feet. She must have been in a room with carpet. The footsteps were soft but firm, possibly male. She breathed, it's all that she could do, but she feared what was to come.

The veil lifted.

TEA TIME

She was not alone. She was still unsure as to who "we" is, but once the hood was lifted, she started to see her surroundings. The light coming in the window was muted by rain. The room she was in was beautifully decorated with dark hues and antiquities that should be in a museum. It looked like they were in a private library. She looked back out the window a bit more closely. There was artificial light as well, but it wasn't enough to hide their location—they weren't in Alexandria, Egypt. *Those are conifer pine trees. Where the hell are we?!*

There was a man holding the hood, his back was turned, face hidden behind the shadows of a hooded sweater. He was heading to the other seated and hooded individual. But she didn't have to see the face, she knew those dirtied up red combat style Doc Martin's.

***

A dark-haired man stood, back to the gagged women in the library, facing the window. He enjoyed the view, always had, ever since the first time he stared out of this window. Dressed in a pair of dress shoes, a clean pin-striped pair of slacks and light blue button-down shirt. He centered his Windsor-knotted neck tie as he turned. There was no reason to look uncivilized for his introduction. He brushed a strand of his dark hair back, it was starting to grey at the temple, but he liked the look.

"Ladies," He looked straight at the older of the two. Though events had taken her away from him, time had not touched her. He remembered her fondly. Her eyes widened as a sudden looked of realization washed over her. She struggled a bit with her restraints. He put one hand in his pocket and took a step casually forward as though this were an everyday occurrence, "Let me introduce myself, I am William Pritcherson."

***

Alexandria's worst nightmare was looking straight at her. A secret that she had held so close to the vest she never thought it would ever be seen by the light of day. Not only was it about to be seen but he was here. She hadn't seen him since she ran from him. Alena was never supposed to know. No amount of good clothing or fine things would ever hide this demon of a man that smiled at her. She struggled against her restraints desperately. Alexandria wanted nothing more than to leave this place with Alena.

William motioned to the person behind her, he released the gag from her mouth, and he then moved Alena to do the same. Once the man finished, he stood quietly, distancing himself from Alena. Alexandria finally got a really good look at the young man in a t-shirt, ratty jeans and a pain of rubber-soled sneakers. Peter, the young intern working with Nadene. *Oh god Nadene!* She hadn't really thought about her until that moment. Alexandria prayed she was alive and safe. What was he doing here, but then she looked back at William and it hit her. The resemblance was too much to be sheer coincidence.

She realized that Alena was watching her, "Alena don't believe anything he says. He's a liar and a vicious man. Why did you bring us here? What do you want, you snake?"

"Such violence for a first love?"

"You ruined me. I ran from you, your cruelty, and hatred. I never loved you. My father didn't want to listen until it was too late. You wouldn't even let me talk to him. Instead you drugged me and threatened me…and far worse, unspeakable things. You are an animal and belong nowhere but a cage." Tears were beginning to stream down her face as she screamed at him in fury.

"Mom stop, please." Alena pleaded. She turned to the man, William, "What do you want with us?"

"Actually, it's not what I want it's what he wants. I am just a facilitator. A keeper for guarding the truth. Peter, why don't you say something, my boy."

Alexandria's fear turned to horror as she realized who Peter actually was and what he may have become after coming into contact with this man. When Peter didn't say anything, but looked at William, Alena chimed in.

"What are you talking about? Are you saying that you are the keeper that left us the note? The person who taunted us with killing friends to lure us for a— conversation?! It sounds like you are the one with the problem even though we are strapped to the chairs."

"I wouldn't taunt anyone here, girl." William growled. "Adara, tell her to stop talking or something less pleasant than this will happen to her."

Adara?! Did he just call her mom Adara? "Adara?" Alena whispered.

Her mother's eyes looked at her with love but beneath the surface was a fear she had never seen. She didn't deny the name. William went behind the desk next to the window, opened a draw and placed a gun on the desk.

"It wasn't an idle threat, young lady." His voice sounded so hollow in his statement.

"Alena, you know, no matter what, I love you."

Alena nodded her headed taking a hint and not wanting to set off the bomb in a tie.

"Well, since my son won't elaborate as to why you are here, I will." William cleared his throat and loaded the gun as he began a tale that started some thirty years ago. Thirty-five years ago, William and Adara had been gently shoved together by her father. William was an up-and-coming businessman in one of her father's companies that he ran when he was not in parliament. At the time, William had made an attractive offer of marriage but something about his temper and somewhat loose morals turned Adara away. She tried to explain to her father, but before she was able to tell her father, William confronted Adara. This confrontation took place while he was visiting after work at the Benakis family home. No one was home but Adara, it was the servant's day off, and Adara had come home a day early from school while the rest of the family was out. The confrontation started as a conversation but became violent. William had hit her hard enough that she landed on the floor in the parlor room. In such a rage, he took the one thing she had continued to deny him: he raped her.

When her family found her, William was long gone, and she did not have the nerve to tell the truth. She said she had fallen down the staircase. It wasn't until a month later that the true horror was revealed to her: she was pregnant.

The next time she saw him, she had made all the arrangements, she was supposed to be going back to school and finish her degree in international studies and law. She was leaving England. He didn't like that. He drugged her tea during their meeting, while she had stepped away for a moment as her father was leaving on another business trip. She then revealed to him that she was pregnant, and the drug took fast effect. He took her. He traveled with her to his place, here actually, in this library. He told her to get rid of the baby or no matter how long it took he would find her. Saying he had powerful friends in places that she didn't even know existed. Then he returned her to her home before anyone suspected her missing. She left without hesitation, and he never heard from her again.

"You didn't hear from me because I never wanted to hear your voice again." Adara said.

"Why did you leave me, mother?" Peter finally spoke.

The shock of his voice made Adara pause, "Peter, I didn't leave you, I was not in a place that I could care for you. I wanted to give you the best chance possible. It wasn't your fault." She paused, catching her breath, Alena got the sense she had never said any of this out loud, "Your birth was so violent that the doctors said I would never conceive again if I lived through it. I didn't think I was going to live. I came back to England when you were due and after living through it I left," Adara looked straight at Peter. No begging or fear in her eyes but the truth. She wasn't going to hide anything. "I wanted you to have the best I could give you, so I gave you to a family, your father didn't want you to begin with."

"Then how did you have her?" Peter considered.

"I didn't," Adara said in a matter of fact tone.

"I am adopted," Alena offered.

"Not exactly. You see when I did in fact live through the birth and was in recovery, Peter was already in the system and in consideration for adoption. I had to go underground. I had to change everything. I couldn't let my family live with my shame, it was my burden to bare. The scandal could have destroyed my father's career." Adara sighed, recollecting the pain of that time, "So, I stayed in the United States. Back then it was somewhat easy to forge documents and build a new identity. I had a couple of university art major friends, at the beginning of my college years, create me some identification documents for one of my projects that was never actually turned in." She shrugged and continued "These documents I had used to change identities, to do things on my own without my family name. So, I changed my name legally and everything. I re-entered university to finish my degree and got my master's and doctorate while I could. I used up a fair amount of the trust fund my father had released to me years prior. That is when I met your father, Alena."

Adara turned to face William, very pointedly said, "He was a *man*."

"How am I not adopted?" Alena didn't know any of this about the woman she called mom, but she still needed an answer.

"You're my niece. I raised you with your fath— uncle I guess is what he actually is."

"What?" Alena breathed.

"You see, your mother was pregnant, when she found me. She attended the same school that I did, she said it was a way for her to cope. But she found my contact information, under one of the old aliases I used to escape the press. But that was another life. She was worried about her pregnancy and wanted me to be your godmother in the event that anything ever happened to her or her husband, your father."

"So, she died in childbirth, well, then what happened to my father." Alena assumed.

"No, your mother lived through childbirth. She was visiting with you. She was an English diplomat at the time, and we were going to meet your uncle for dinner, your parents picked me up from the house in Los Angeles. On the way, they were shot. Gratefully, I had you in my arms. They didn't even make it to the hospital." The memory of violence and loss brought a new set of tears to Adara's eyes. She paused after a moment and swallowed her tears, "after the legal paperwork, the next day you were ours. You were just a few weeks old. But your mother had named you, and we kept you just as you came to us."

Alena's head was swirling with the information. She wasn't really adopted, and she was in fact living with family her whole life. This information changed everything and yet nothing, but she couldn't focus on that now. One question popped into mind "Do you know who killed my parents?"

"At the time, they said it was a terrorist attack, but it was too clean and professional. It was too focused, only two bullets were found at the scene, one for each of their targets." Adara looked straight at the man who had turned his back and moved to sit in the plush chair behind the desk. "I never could prove it, but I always felt *you* had something to do with it."

"How dare you accuse him. I'm tired of your lies. My father has done nothing but good for society. The world isn't always ready for the truth or the knowledge that the world gives. HE makes sure what is given is enough of the truth to believe, he is a powerful and burdened man." Peter defended this man, and he believed the words that he said but he was troubled by Adara's words. Peter had completed the training in record time for the Keepers. There were somethings about the story that he was unsure of but he defended him.

"Peter, that's not necessary." William got up and moved towards Adara. He stopped short and leaned in to her cheek and whispered so softly in her ear, "I missed my target. Those bullets were meant for you, you took my son from me, I didn't want you getting in the way of my finding him. I did call the hit on all of you, but you were supposed to die on the scene. When he missed I killed him."

Chapter XXIII

Alena was reeling, with the recent revelations she had solved the cold case. *It was too clean, though*, she thought, *something is missing, but I am not sure what*. If they lived through this, she had a very important phone call to make. Alena looked to her now aunt and didn't care about the truth coming out. She wished it had come out differently but now that it was out, she was simply glad to know it. The next step was to get out of here, but how, was the problem. She wondered if she had remembered to put her tiny pocket knife in the secret pocket of her holster, that was still fastened across her chest. She wouldn't even know until these zip-ties were cut. Alena was in a catch-22. She didn't even have her gun, Peter had it. She could see her gun's grip sticking out of his pants. For his sake, she hoped the safety was on.

There was a long pause after William Pritcherson walked back and sat at his desk. "Where are my manners? It's been hours since you have been here, and I haven't even asked you to dinner. Ladies, would you like something to eat and perhaps drink? Who am I kidding, with this company and my selection of food, you would be a fool not to accept."

He opened a drawer in the desk pulled out a pair of scissors and a roll of duct tape and slowly walked towards Adara. He kneeled down and slowly lifted her pant leg, cut the zip-tie and repeated the action to the other leg. Alena couldn't quiet tell but she thought she saw a sneer spread across his face. He handed the scissors to Peter who stood there motionless for a moment. William paused for a moment, when Peter did nothing, he took the scissors back. He handed Peter the duct tape and pointed to Adara, "Wrap her wrists and cover her mouth." Peter walked to do so as William walked towards Alena and reached to touch her cheek. Alena turned away.

"Don't you touch her" Adara said with such a tone that everyone there knew it was not an empty threat. William slowly removed his hand and walked back to Adara.

"I am glad you haven't lost your fire, Adara." He grabbed the roll of duct tape that was now laying on the ground. He peeled a piece off and placed it over her mouth, he lingered on her cheek and kissed the tape where her lips would have been.

211

"Stop it! Leave her alone you creep." Alena screamed.

Peter walked back to Alena and cut the zip-ties on her right ankle and held it in place, so she wouldn't kick him. He leaned up to her ear, "Stop. Don't show your emotions. I have a plan, this isn't what I wanted, I am sorry."

Alena didn't say anything, but their eyes met, and she felt he was sincere. She stopped struggling as Peter cut the other zip-tie to her ankle. He rolled her shirt sleeves down and then grabbed the duct tape from his father.

"What are you doing?" William said.

"I was going to duct tape her hands together… so they couldn't escape after we sit them down to dinner?" replied Peter in a confident yet confused voice as he shrugged his shoulders.

"Thank you for following directions."

Peter cut the zip-ties one at a time. Quickly, with his strong hands, grabbed both of Alena's wrists and wrapped them in duct tape over her sleeves. He tossed it back to his father, who caught it without looking away from Adara, and was hand-given the scissors. William carefully grabbed her legs before cutting the zip-ties, fearing as Peter did that Adara would use her legs against him. He taped her wrists together and lifted her easily out of the chair. Peter offered his hand to Alena. Instead of touching him at all she got out of the chair on her own and waited. She waited to be led somewhere or for this to turn into some sick joke, she wasn't sure.

Peter put tape over Alena's mouth before they were guided out of the room and down the hall to a room that was reasonably comfortable. It was too small to be a bedroom but maybe another study or dressing room, it didn't matter to the pair of women they just wanted to get away from here. They heard the door lock as the men closed the door when they left. Alena walked to Alexandria before she had the chance to bang on the door. She motioned and grabbed the tape on her face and pulled, "Ouch." Alexandria did the same for her, "Ow! Well, at least it's not as bad at painter's tape." Alexandria turned and stared at Alena, "What I was curious as a kid which tape hurt the most when ripped off, I was very bored."

Shaking her head, "Okay, so how do we get out of here?"

Alena looked out the window, "It is too tall a jump for that to work, but maybe—" as she noticed some linens, "here can you help me get this tape off my wrists?"

"Of cour—" she was cut off with the sound of the door. It hadn't been but a few minutes when they heard the lock click in the door.

"Shit!" Alena breathed out just a Peter appeared in the doorway. "What do you want?" looking for something to throw.

Peter stood there, unsurprised that they had removed the tape, "I see you can talk. Good, come mother, father wants to see you."

"Over my dead body," she spat on the carpet and stood there, firm like a strong-rooted tree.

Peter pulled out a gun from his pocket, Alena's gun, and clicked off the safety, "Don't make this any more difficult than it is."

Alena grabbed the hand of the woman who raised her. Alexandria gripped her hands and removed them. "I'll go," she walked towards Peter, "Just remember I tried to do right by you, I gave you life, I am your mother, and that man is a monster. He is a liar. Please Peter. Walk away and if you can't save me, save Alena and yourself."

Without a word he motioned with the gun for her to move. She hesitated but moved. "Peter—" Alena tried to say, but he pointed the gun at her in silence. He closed the door and locked it again, she could hear his and Alexandria's footsteps recede.

"Son of a—" she put the tape on her wrists to her mouth and started ripping the tape with her teeth.

***

Dr. Jansen walked out of the ruins in the underground and back to the dig site tents. The sun was just kissing the horizon of dawn against the dunes. Kendra and Sita were walking on their own and breathing more comfortably, but Nadene knew they still needed to go to the hospital. She grabbed the satellite phone that was on the table and her first call was to the local hospital. She explained the situation and that she was keeping a very sharp eye on both women, with confirmation that a couple paramedics were on the way, she hung up.

She went back to tending to Sita and Kendra and making sure that they were lying down, staying calm, before the paramedics came. She then had the urge to call Alena and Alexandria, knowing full well that neither were likely to pick up the phone, especially if her suspicions were true. Nadene dialed Alexandria's number first…straight to voicemail. Then she tried Alena's … it rang once…twice…and three times before going to voicemail. She left a message but hung up hoping one good thing: they had a phone. She could hear a set of tires coming across the road to the tents. She turned and saw the paramedics, she had to handle one crisis before she could help Alex and Alena. But the moment Kendra and Sita

215

were taken care of she would be able to make her move. She texted the team group chat to let everyone know what was going on, and so she could see who would respond. After a couple minutes only one number didn't respond, the intern Peter.

Nadene dialed the number she knew was Joey Blake, "Joey, when was the last time you saw Peter?"

"Sometime late last night, he took his shift and then texted around four this morning that he had shifted with another member of the team, why?"

"Peter didn't respond to the text and Dr. Martin and Alena are missing. Who switched with him?"

"I don't know he said it was an intern but there wasn't a name, I am already checking the message," realizing the severity of the situation he is now privy to.

"Joey, text me his number, I will call him directly and find out where he is, I need to eliminate my suspicions."

"Suspicions?"

"I don't know but I fear he is more involved in Alex and Alena's disappearance."

"What?" Surprise woke Joey up, faster than a strong espresso. "What do you mean disappearance?"

"I'll explain, but I need you to start the process of emergency contacts: Head of Antiquities, police…you have a copy of the list."

"Yeah, sure, let me know if I can help."

"I will," Dr. Nadene Jansen heard her phone ping with a text message. Joey had sent her Peter's number.

Chapter XXIV

With the last of the duct tape peeled off, Alena was able to feel her hands again. She rolled her sleeves up as she was looking for a way out. She grabbed the linens and reached into her holster for the small pocket knife. *YES! It was still there.* She opened it and cut at a corner. She was going to tie a rope together from the shredded linen and get down to the next window or the ground. She had to get out, it didn't matter how but she had to save her family.

She had to rip the linen quietly yet with haste. She finished a rope that was a couple sheets long, she looked for something to tie it on. There wasn't a bed post or furniture heavy enough to hold her weight. "Shit," she breathed.

***

Alexandria heard the door behind her lock. The room was huge, well-furnished and filled with items to show extravagance, a gilded cage. She wasn't bothered so much by the stuff or the feeling of claustrophobia, but by the voice that she suddenly heard. "Adara, I would like to ... retry this."

Alexandria stood rooted next to the door. She didn't move or utter a word. William was laying on the bed leaving little to the imagination. He was wearing a green and gold smoking jacket loosely tied around his waist, exposing a hairy chest and designer boxer-briefs. She saw the gun on the bed between her and him. Their eyes met. Hers were daggers filled with a hatred so strong it heated the room. He slinked off the bed in his robe and walked towards her. She didn't move, and she didn't speak, not even a flinch when he touched her arm. She waited for the right moment. He grabbed her wrist and began to remove the tape.

"Don't try anything, the gun is within arms-reach," William stated as he kissed her hands and gripped at the slightest resistance.

Alexandria felt the pain in her wrist and could feel her skin prickle at his touch, she wanted to hit him. He guided her closer to the bed, she pulled back. "Adara, play nicely."

"No" She swiftly lifted her knee, but he moved out of the way. His retaliation was swift and painful like a rehearsed reaction. He bent her wrist and she landed off balance on her knees crying out in pain. He twisted her wrist and arm behind her back, William smiled when she cried out.

"I told you not to try anything, now I can't play nice, that just wouldn't be fair. Turn over,"

"I can't, you idiot,"

He twisted again.

"Ah! Alright, alright" She slowly turned to her back so that she wouldn't twist her arm any further. "What is all this, there wasn't this pretense when you raped me last time."

"I wanted you willingly," he growled as he unbuttoned her shirt one-handed. He lowered his face to her neck, she turned away. He stopped unbuttoning and grabbed her face, turned it forward to kiss her on the lips. She closed her eyes, knowing that Alena was a few doors down, but she couldn't scream. A single tear fell down her face as he went back to the buttons. She was going to have to think her way out of this.

She didn't resist his touch but turned away again, praying for a moment to land her knee between his legs.

***

     Alena tied her linen rope to the cabinet that was at the back corner of the room and tugged, still unsure if it would hold for as long as she needed. She put her little knife in her holster and grabbed the linen. Detective Martin opened the window and tossed it down and out the window frame. It stopped just above the ground. She grabbed the second linen rope she made and tied it to the doorknob. This rope would act as her safety and back-up. Wrapping the second rope tightly around her waist, she grabbed a hold of both and gripped tightly. She climbed over the railing and prayed.

     When she realized she hadn't fallen, and her fear of heights hadn't kicked in yet, she breathed. She climbed down the ropes a step at a time. She got to the window below the room she was in—it was closed and locked. "Well, damn." In a moment of pure impulse, she held on to the rope and propelled herself against the wall and tried to aim for the window. Alena aimed for the window with her side and brought her knees in, for as much protection against glass as she could get. She saw the window come closer she tightened her grip and closed her eyes. Alena heard the glass shatter as she hit the floor. She stayed put for a moment before she opened her eyes. *Good, it was in*

221

fact empty, no one hiding next to the window or waiting for me, she thought.

Brushing off the glass she felt a tinge of pain in her left arm and side. A small shard of glass was protruding from her bicep and thigh. She didn't have a choice, she had to pull them out, but she had nothing to treat them with…wait. The rope.

She looked around for anything she could use to grab it. By the small fireplace there was a poker. She grabbed it with her right hand and reached through the sharp waves of pain. Finally, she was able to get it close enough to grab. Alena brought in as much of the linen as she could get into the room. She had to move quickly, someone surely heard the crash. Grabbing her small knife, she cut a few pieces big enough to wrap around the wounds as bandages. She grabbed the glass and carefully pulled it out of her arm, trying not to scream. She bit her lip, breaking the delicate skin of the lower lip with the pain. Quickly, Alena applied pressure and tied the linen around her arm as she breathed out. She repeated these steps methodically with her thigh. She tied both wraps as tight as she could stand it. Another shirt stained with her blood that she would have to replace later. *At this rate I'll be out of shirts by Christmas*, she thought.

Alena pulled herself up and put some of her weight on her leg but shifted most of it to her right foot as she walked to the door. She noticed something shiny on the wall. It was a knife, a good-sized hunting knife. *Rather be armed than sorry*, she thought. She grabbed the knife off of the wall and twisted the doorknob. It was unlocked. Cautiously she opened the door, opening a couple inches at first, and then peeking her head out. The hall was clear.

Walking out, she quietly rushed up through the hall when she heard footsteps coming towards her. Down the staircase the footfalls came, she looked for a place to hide, but couldn't find any. She ducked behind a dresser in the hall a couple yards ahead of her and waited to surprise the would-be assailant with the knife. She heard a gun cock. She assumed he would be armed, but she had just brought a knife to a gun fight.

***

Alexandria heard a crash of glass, just as William was pulling her shirt off. She knew she didn't have a lot of time, but his attention faltered for a second, long enough to maybe get out of his grasp. Alexandria twisted out of his grip and pulled away from him trying to get up off the floor. He came after her, he smacked her across the face.

Hard, the blow forced her to her knees, as she landed back on the floor. A small amount of blood trickled of her mouth; she had bitten her cheek when she was struck. Alexandria lifted herself but was met by the pressure of his hand at her neck.

"No! Let go!" She cried out, she hoped it had been Alena that crashed in the window. William moved his hand to the front of her neck. She had managed a cry before he choked the second in her throat.

Alena heard a cry and then another more muffled. She had to get to her mom. She jumped out and stabbed someone, she heard a wet sound as the knife entered flesh and a cry of pain before she looked up to see her assailant's face. "Peter?!" he cried in pain as his response. "Give me my gun" When Peter hesitated, she twisted the knife into his lower right leg, until he dropped her gun.

"Thank you." Alena picked up her gun and holstered it before she pulled out the knife. Peter crumpled on the floor grasping for his bloody shin.

"I was coming to help you,"

"I don't need your help, but why do you bother"

"Because this is wrong, I am sorry"

"You're too little too late, jackass," Alena grabbed the knife and held it to his throat, "How do I get out of here? What was your plan?"

"There is a car out front with a full tank, get to the airport and report to the embassy." Peter said through clenched teeth.

"Embassy? Why would I need to talk to the embassy, where are we?"

"You're in France" he shifted his weight.

"Son of a bitch! Stay on the floor"

"Wait, take me with you,"

"What?! No, you nearly got me killed, and now you're an accessory to rape or god only knows what else he is doing to my mother. If you had a shred of decency you would stay right here and wait for the authorities once we are out of the house." When he didn't answer she applied a bit of pressure to the knife that was resting on his neck. "Okay"

He nodded his head, "I'll tell the truth"

"Good, because if you lie, there will be hell to pay, do you understand?"

He nodded his head one more time. She lifted the knife and eyed him one last time before getting up looking at the staircase. "You remind me of my sister." Peter said, as he stared at Alena Martin. She slowly backed away, ignoring him.

She heard another cry out, a bit more muffled than the last couple, and she rushed to the door that she heard it coming from. Even through the pain she nearly ran, she stopped to put the knife carefully in her belt and to pull her gun back out. She twisted the doorknob. Locked, she suspected as much but was still hoping she wasn't going to have to use her body to slam against the door.

She braced herself and rammed her right side against the door…twice…three times before she felt the door give way. William Pritcherson was on top of Alexandria Martin, in a struggle, back to the door. Alena couldn't tell how far that struggle had gone but she did see her mother's pants were still on. "Hey, dick," she cocked the gun "you have until I count to three to get off her. 1…" he continued to struggle with her mother, "2…" Alexandria elbowed him in the chest as an attempt to get him off "3…" She fired two rounds, one in his leg and the other in his ass.

"I am sorry you didn't take me seriously," she said as he cried out in pain and rolled onto his back. "But I did warn you." Alena kept her gun trained on the man in his smoking jacket now bleeding all over the floor. She walked over to her mother, stretched out her injured arm to help her up. Alena cringed. She knew her mother would see the pain, she would get help later, after dealing with this monster.

"You, bitch!"

"Ah that's not very kind language towards a woman with a gun pointed at you." Alena for one moment let herself feel the anger, the pure hatred for the man, as she held her hand steady with her finger hovering at the trigger. She took a deep breath, a fierce sense of déjà vu washing over her senses. The adrenaline surged through her veins, as everything seemed to sharpen. Alena breathed again and steadied her hand as she pulled her mother behind her and walked out of the door backwards. Hovering at the door, she thought for one moment, aimed, and fired her gun. The bullet went into the wood next to his ear but didn't hit him. He definitely will have ringing in his ears for a while. "Mr. Pritcherson, I want you to know how close you came to death tonight. I want you to know that you will never see us again, and I want you to know that you will never see the light of day again, I will make sure of that." The look on his face was enough to make her smile as she walked out the door.

***

Nadene had tried calling Peter earlier, but she didn't think it could hurt again. About two more hours had gone by before she thought of Alex and Alena again. Two hours of policy and emergency phone calls to almost a dozen

individuals. Kendra and Sita were safely on the way to the
hospital, Joey rode with them. The team had all shown up
within about thirty minutes after her group message, Joey
being the first to arrive.

"Joey, I am so grateful you are here," Nadene said
as he got out of the front seat of rental car for the team to
carpool with.

"My God, Dr. Jansen, are you okay? What
happened?" he said as he reached for her. They embraced
for a moment.

"I am, the girls are too, but the paramedics are on
the way just to be sure," Nadene said as she walked back to
the tent, Joey following from behind as the other members
of the team got out of the car.

"What can I do then?"

"I need you to ride with them, make sure they get
there. I have to find out what happened to Alex and Alena."
Nadene said keeping the fear from creeping into her voice.

Joey had been her assistant partner, and now friend
for a couple years. He had his master's degree in
engineering, they met a couple years ago when his advisor
sent her his thesis on experimental engineering for
archaeology. She was in meetings for funds at the time, but
this came up and she was intrigued at the use of
S.E.S.A.M.E. He could have a teaching position himself if

he chose to, but he wanted to work on his doctorate with Nadene Jansen as his mentor in Archaeological Engineering. She had agreed to be his mentor, not because she felt obligated but because she was happy to help a friend learn as much in his passion as she could.

She pulled her phone out of her back pocket. She would have to be fast, her cellphone was dying. As she dialed the number for Peter, the screen went black.

"Damn it, I will have to use the satellite phone."

She walked back into the tent, picked up the phone off of its bulky charger. It had half a charge, that should be enough for a few phone calls. She would start with Peter and finish following up with the rest of the contacts on the list of emergency contacts.

***

Peter was gripping his leg still on the floor when he felt his phone vibrate. He reached for the phone in his pocket and swiped the lock screen, "Yes," he answered. He could hear the voice on the other line was familiar and then he recognized it.

"Peter, I need to know the truth. Where are you?"

"I'm in France."

"Do you know where Alex and Alena are?"

"My mother and her daughter are here."

"What? Nevermind, I'll find out later. Peter, that doesn't help me. Why are they in France? I need to know where they are specifically?"

"They are in danger—" He heard the gun fire in the room above him. He didn't know who had been shot but he knew he was now in a lot of trouble with a lot of people. "Nadene, I need you to call the embassy."

"Embassy, which embassy?"

"The American or English Embassy in France."

"What kind of danger are they in?" Nadene said the fear cracking her voice.

"Just trust me for one second, they are in serious danger, they need your help, I need you to call the embassy, they will get here faster than anyone else." He hung up the phone and put it back in his pocket.

He would have to save his own skin on this one. Releasing his leg, he reached into the left pocket with his second phone. He dialed the only number he had saved on this phone. The dial tone rang only once, "Hello,"

Peter remembered the voice as the man he met a few years ago at the party, "Sir, this is Peter Pritcherson, we have a situation and I need some help from the Keepers."

Alexandria walked out of the door and waited for a moment to catch her breath. Alena walked over the door and stood next to her, "Mom, we have to go, we can't wait, someone surely heard the gunfire, even from here."

"I know, I just needed a second."

"Mom, are you okay?" Alena's tone of voice changed very quickly when she saw her mother's face. She had never seen such fear in her mother's eyes.

"I will be, it just brought back…"

"I know, let's get out of here and we will talk, okay?"

Alexandria nodded her head, breathed. She knew she had to move but at that moment it was one of the hardest things to do. She turned her back on the man who caused her so much pain for the last time. They walked down the stairs, Alena leaning on her mother for support. Her strength was leaving her, seeping into the linen bandage. Peter was on the floor bleeding.

"Peter—"

"Leave him, he will be fine, the authorities need to find him."

"But he is bleeding,"

"I know, it's not life-threatening." Alena turned to Peter, "Hey, where did you put my phone," she raised her gun and aimed at his leg just to be sure.

"It's in the bowl by the door." He said without hesitation.

"It there a landline?"

He nodded and tilted his head down, "In the room to the left, its an old rotary."

"Good."

Alena headed down the hall, she could feel fresh blood seeping into the linen wraps. She had to get to a hospital, fast. She heard her mother follow behind her. Alena grabbed the phone, just inside the doorway and dialed the emergency number in France. Grateful at this moment for the international safety class she took years ago. She heard a pleasant male voice come on the line,

"Quelle est la nature de votre urgence?"

"S'il vous plait. Parlez vous anglaise?"

"Yes, how can I help?"

"Can you tell me where I am, track the call? I have been attacked and I am losing blood—" Alena's head started to spin. She had lost enough blood that she was disoriented. "I need the embassy" she gripped the wall for balance but couldn't stabilize.

"Alena!" Her mother screamed as she ran towards her. Alena had collapsed to her right knee.

"I am okay I just need a second, I need you to talk to them." She nodded her head. In near perfect French, Alexandria explained what they needed to know about the situation, emphasizing and why they needed the embassy.

"Merci, s'il vous plait faites vite. We will meet an authority at the hospital" Alexandria Martin stated.

"Stay where you are, please" the calm male voice said over the phone.

"No, I know where I am, and I can get her there faster." was the last thing Alexandria said, not giving the operator time to answer. She hung up the receiver. Alena was catching her breath leaning up against the wall. They walked out of the room, but Alena had to stop she was slipping into unconsciousness. She propelled herself off the wall and started to walk, only to falter to her knees again in the hallway.

"Alena, come with me, give me your hand, we are headed to the hospital, I am afraid of the blood loss."

"I'm okay," She lied, and Alexandria knew it.

"No, you're not, now give me your hand,"

Alena lifted her head and gave her right hand to Alexandria. She was half-way to standing when she felt a new pain wash through her left shoulder. She knew this type of pain—it was a bullet. She heard a second gunshot and saw the bullet fly past her and hit the wooden wall.

"Faaa—" Alena cried out and partially collapsed in on herself. She felt her arm and back sear with pain. Alena dropped from her mother's support, landing on her back. Clenching her teeth, she tried to breathe through the bone cracking pain. The bullet had hit her shoulder blade, she could feel the bullet in her muscles. Alexandria lifted her daughter all the way to her feet, grabbed the Glock 19, still in Alena's right hand and turned. She heard William's gun click with an empty magazine, "Shit."

Alexandria fired three bullets. Alena saw the last bullet meet a rather poetic target through the staircase railing, just as they turned back towards the door. Alexandria put the weapon in its holster and carried much of the weight of Alena as they made their way towards the door. The last thing Alena remembered was grabbing her cell-phone from the bowl at the door and putting it in her pocket.

***

What must have been hours later, Alena woke up with a jerk and a startling amount of pain in her whole body. "Shit, I haven't felt this much pain since that time I broke my arm in seventh grade. My last bullet wasn't this bad." She mustered a small chuckle, as she noticed her mother, "Well, by the look on your face, I'd gather that what just happened was real and I am going to have a couple of scars,"

"Yes, but your will make a full recovery, the bullet hit your shoulder blade. The doctors were able to pull in all out. It just chipped your lower shoulder blade hitting mostly muscle, thank god."

Alena looked around a bit dazed and realized she was in a hospital bed, which explained the stiff mattress beneath her. Her arm and thigh were dressed properly, she could feel the stitches beneath the gauze on all three injures. Her arm was the most uncomfortable pain, but she knew it would heal given rest and time. She was not looking forward to a new round of physical therapy. There was a tray of food on her bedside table.

"Food? How long was I out?"

"Several hours,"

"What happened, I don't remember getting here." The smell of the still-warm roll reaching her nostrils. She knew it had been awhile since either of them had eaten. She made a reach for the food but cringed in pain.

"Use your words, I am here," Alexandria said as she reached to put the injured girl back in the bed, gently placing a hand on her left arm. She grabbed the table and moved it closer so as to help her eat.

"Have you heard from Nadene?"

"Yes, I called her once we were on the way to the hospital. The girls are in a hospital in Alexandria," the cell-phone in Alexandria's lap pinged with a notification, "and it would seem Nadene has landed at the airport, she's on her way."

"I was out that long, huh?"

"I'm glad you haven't lost your sense of humor," She smiled.

Alena hadn't seen her smile in what felt like years, "Oh do you want any of this, I am so hungry that this hospital food smells like a feast at Valhalla," putting the roll in her mouth.

"I will have Nadene stop for a couple sandwiches, how about that?"

"Deal." Alena smiled and glad she didn't actually have to eat the hospital food.

The Recovery

Chapter XXV

Jack Wills had gotten out of his rental car and put his sanitary latex-free gloves on each hand. Interpol agent Wills walked into one of the most extravagant houses he had ever seen. There was a semi-level, a U-shaped landing that an intricate staircase led up to. He felt as though he was walking into a museum, everything was restored to its former glory of the French baroque style. Filigree in the corners of the golden crown molding, decorative embellishments on the staircases, walls painted in rich gemstone hues, painted glass in the windows, rugs imported from all over the East and centuries old, but no one could tell as the pigments were as bright as the day they were made. Several other agents from the embassies of France, England and the United States had already shown up. He hadn't been from his desk in a while and was grateful for a chance for field work.

"Oh, hey Jacks, how's it feel to be back in the field?" his friend and long-time partner John Baxter called from inside the house.

"It's pretty odd actually, I had gotten accustomed to the paperwork." Wills chuckled and shrugged, "I'm sorry I am late, they wanted me to meet with the victims at the hospital a few miles away from here. Gratefully, they're both alive but one was bloody as hell."

"We heard she was in rough shape when she got there, I asked the nurse if you were there yet and you were. You always had a better bedside manner than anyone here."

"Thanks, the older woman was assaulted and nearly raped, but the younger wasn't able to speak. She was suffering from massive blood loss from three injuries and trauma. Let's find out what happened here and get these bastards."

"So, you only have one account, from the women I mean, right?"

"Yea, but I am going to go back, I asked the doctor to call me when they are ready."

"Good, oh hey, weren't you going back to Scotland Yard?"

"Yes, I'd like to go home maybe retire, change careers, the death is a burden that I never anticipated,"

"I don't blame you, get out while you still have your sanity. Don't go numb here, find a girl while you're still young, and remember what good coffee tastes like."

"I drink tea at the office," Jack Wills smiled wryly.

"I know that, but you know what I mean, yea?"

"Yes, I do, and thank you."

Jack Wills walked through the house and the first thing he noticed, aside from the indulgence in architecture, was a small pool of blood by the stairs with a bullet hole imbedded in the wooden wall of the hallway. There was a bloody partial handprint on the top of a cabinet next to a glass bowl near the front door. He saw a body on the upper lading and another larger pool of blood. The amount of blood in a pool further down the hall could have killed someone but there was no second body. Jack Wills new he had his work cut out for him and probably several blood-types to match. He walked up the staircase carefully watching the forensics team brush and swab every little grain and drop of blood in the house. He made his way to the open door on the landing hallway. There were a number of police officers hovering in the doorway speaking French. He never liked it when someone spoke another language in an attempt to avoid speaking or hide the fact that they did in fact speak English.

"Bonjour, si vous n'allez pas aider, vous êtes sur le chemin." He said in his broken French, "Merci," he said as they haughtily walked out of the door.

"Hey, so we have a bit of a mess," chief of Interpol Forensics, Agent Parker said.

"Yes, I can see that. Can you give me anything more than that?"

Joana Parker was a woman of brilliance, her deep brown eyes seemed to read a person and a room like a radar. Jack Wills never could hide a thing from her. They were good friends and had stayed in touch even after she left Scotland Yard for Interpol. He was only temporarily assigned to the joint task force to help with this case; it matched a case with a similar MO in London.

"Well, actually, there is something funny."

"Oh yeah, what have you found?" Wills said eager to get any kind of lead on this bloody mess.

"Well this man didn't die of the multiple gunshot wounds, had he made it to hospital, he might have lived, they were all superficial flesh wounds, scaring but not mortal. But there is one here," she pointed to the massive exposed trauma that was once his neck, "that is what killed him, nearly severely his head, and it's a different gun entirely, I found shot gun pellets. Whoever shot this last round wanted to make sure he would never talk again."

TEA TIME

Jack Wills looked as close as he dared before he could feel what he ate of his dinner in the back of his throat. He nodded his head. The woman in the hospital didn't kill this man. She was being framed for it.

***

Peter Pritcherson had passed out after making the phone call to the Keepers. If he couldn't save his bastard of a father, he was going to save himself. He had been lied to, his mother had wanted the best for him, not his liar of a father. It was his chance to walk away from this mess and become his own keeper. He wanted to rip the Keepers apart. They had all lied to him. Yet again he was being taken advantage of. The honest ones were Alena and his mother. Alena reminded him so much of Sonja, her will to never surrender stirred his brotherly instincts that he had suppressed for so long. He hadn't seen Sonja since her high school graduation, but he loved her and would protect her fiercely. When Alena was on top of him, knife to his throat, he could sense the truth in her eyes. Her fierce eyes. Peter was overwhelmed with the urge to protect her: she was, in fact, family if everything were true. He gave her the advice to call the embassy. As he laid there on the floor, watching her crumpled body go out the door, he realized the fullness of his mistake. Peter wanted to help her more than just by getting her out of the house and away from William Pritcherson.

The only way he could think of helping was to blow it apart from the inside. He called to get help but also to wash his hands clean of the man lying on the floor ten feet above him. He would expose the story about a secret organization that controls all information from the inside. Peter wasn't sure how he was going to get out of this, but he had to. He realized his entire life for the past several years was an utter lie and now he had to create anew. He might even be able to redeem himself one day.

Peter was gently jarred awake, but only for a moment. That moment was long enough for him to realize he was being carried and then carefully placed into a car. Peter thought he saw the man's face, but he did recognize the voice. The man on the phone came in person.

"Don't worry my son, we are going to take care of you. You will be a full Keeper when you wake."

Peter didn't respond but closed his eyes and fell back to a dreamless sleep. The rage of life-long lies would end, someone had to take the blame. The Keepers had to fall. No one should have the power to completely control and determine what information is available. He would have to do his research, find a weakness, and use it. Peter heard a single shot fired before completely drifting to the abyss of sleep.

***

James Benakis woke up to the sound of his phone ringing, it was probably some board member, he would call them back later. He opened his eyes to see that young female doctor checking his charts again.

"Doctor, what can I do for you?"

"Well, I am hoping to release you tomorrow, after tests yesterday, your vitals are returning to normal and the enzyme that is in cardiac events like yours has dissipated. That being said, I would like to keep you just for the one night. Do you have anyone we need to alert, or maybe come pick you up or…?" Her kind voice reminded him of the young detective he had hired. James was still hoping her fresh eyes would see something he missed and that he would hear something soon. He gave the doctor Detective Martin's number. He wanted the doctor to give Detective Martin a courtesy call.

"Okay, just fine Mr. Benakis, is she a relative?"

"No, she is an acquaintance, but she still ought to know."

"When you call her can I speak with her?"

"Sure, I will call her in a few, since you are awake."

"Thank you."

Doctor Greene walked out after putting his chart back in place. He could hear her heels click outside in the hall towards the nurse's desk. Muffled by distance, the sounds of the building mixed with his aged hearing made, it was difficult to hear the conversation but he did hear part of the exchange, "Oh I am so sorry to hear that, would you care to talk to him on her behalf? … sure, sure I understand…oh no, it's not a problem, he just wanted to speak to her…oh no, that's okay…well, here I will put him on…oh no, that's not a problem at all."

He heard the phone in his room ring and he struggled to reach the receiver, but he managed to pick it up at the second ring. "Hello," James said a bit breathless, "Is this my PI?"

"Mr. Benakis, this is someone who can talk to you on her behalf, I'll give you the line now, let me know if I can help," Doctor Greene's voice said kindly on the line then he heard a faint click, ending the doctor's line.

"James?" That voice. He knew it. It was like a dream, he never thought he would hear that voice again. Adara was on the phone.

"Adara?" he ventured. He checked his pulse and his monitors, thinking he had flatlined in his stretch to the phone.

"It's me, James, I know this must come as a shock after all these years, but I'll catch you up sometime. But for now, just know that both of us are okay, Alena and me."

"Are you sure? Where are you?"

"We are at a hospital in France. Are you still living in the family house?" she asked knowingly.

"How did you--?"

"I kept tabs, but I always knew you would never leave the house, you always liked it more than me or Mariana."

"That is true," he chuckled. "You will have to come visit," he offered trying hard not to pry, just happy to hear her voice.

"I was hoping to, especially after tonight, I hear you're in the hospital too?"

"Yes, I get out tomorrow with any luck."

"Oh good. Umm, I will call when I can."

"I know, I've missed you, so much. I am just happy to hear you."

"It's good to be heard, and I've missed you too. We'll talk soon."

He could hear her voice crack in the last words, but then she hung up before he could say anything else.

***

Nadene Jansen walked in, hands full, to the hospital room. Alexandria was hanging up the phone and Alena was asleep. Nadene dropped the couple bags of takeout into the chair and placed her over-night bag on the ground next to it.

"Who was that?" wondering who Alex could be talking to at this hour.

"I'll tell you later, how was your flight?"

"Quick, which was good. I got your call as I was driving by the deli I come to anytime I visit Parsi. Gratefully, they have crazy hours."

"Then, I guess I had good timing when I called." Alexandria smiled, "What did you get?"

"Well, I wasn't sure what anyone wanted so I picked a couple that I enjoy and a few drinks. The sides were a fruit salad and a green salad, so I got each of us one of each. I figured from your call you two hadn't eaten in a while."

"Not since Alexandria."

"Whoa! That's over thirty-six hours."

247

"Is that all?"

"Well, yea, we went to the ruins, technically two nights ago, if you do the math of time zones." Nadene smirked, remembering how much she forgot to account time by time zones.

"I guess you're right. That's actually almost forty hours altogether." Alexandria reached for a fruit salad. It was simple, fresh cut fruit with a very light yoghurt drizzle. It tasted so good.

"Do you want to wait until she wakes? The food is all cold sandwiches, nothing is warm." Nadene said after unwrapping a sandwich and hesitating. Alena tossed in the sheets and muttered a bit.

"Yes, that way we can make sure she eats something good. She was so hungry before she fell asleep, she ate the roll on the hospital tray."

"Really? She always hated hospital food. If I remember from the visits in the hospital with your husband correctly, she said 'This stuff smells like death and tastes of cardboard.'"

"I remember," Alexandria chuckled as she looked at her daughter. Alena had always had a knack for word uses and even made up words as a child to suit her needs when the dictionary didn't.

"Is she out of the woods yet?" Nadene asked suddenly serious.

"So, to speak, yes. She was in surgery for what seemed like days. But the good thing is that the bullet went through her, muscle and tissue were damaged. The bone stopped it. The doctors found it, whole, lodged in the tip of her shoulder blade. That will make the healing process a bit harder, but they are going to keep her a couple nights as she lost a lot of blood. She'll have physical therapy when we get back to LA and should make a full recovery." Alexandria turned her attention from Nadene to Alena when she heard a whispered name.

"Mom…?"

"I'm right here, Aunt Nada is here too. We have sandwiches if you're are up to it."

Alena's eyes opened.

"My mouth is a little dry…" a tickle in her throat had Alena in a bit of pain and a minor cough. Alexandria quickly grabbed a small paper cup with water and handed it to Alena. Alena carefully gripped the cup and sipped gingerly.

"Better?" Alena nodded her head in response, "Are you hungry?"

"Starved." Alena's voice was starting to sound normal again, a good sign for everyone.

"Sandwich?" Alexandria unwrapped the one marked 'boef' remembering Alena's rare indulgence in her favorite sandwich meat, the sandwich was enveloped in a baguette. "Here, roast beef. It is cold, but it smells great."

Alena took a bite and smiled, "Bread."

Nadene emptied the contents of the brown paper bags on the seat. Alena hadn't realized how hungry she was until she took her second bite. The second bite she actually...tasted. The baguette had that nice crunch in the crust but a chewy aromatic center. If the feeling of comfort had a smell it would be the smell a fresh baguette. She could taste the garlic horseradish, crunchy lettuce and mild cheese. Nadene pulled out biodegradable containers, filled with fresh seasonal fruit and green salads. Small sauce containers had an oil-based dressing. Napkins and forks were pulled out from the bottom. Alena refocused her attention to the smell of roast beef and cheese padded with lettuce and a hint of Dijon mustard on the bottom layer of bread.

"What sandwiches are you eating?" muffled by the food and her hand covering her mouth.

"I think this one is tuna," Alexandria chuckled, "honestly, I am not one-hundred percent, but I like it." She shrugged as she took another bite.

"This is a ham and cheese, nothing complicated, just something comforting," Nadene smiled and wiped the little bit of mustard that had kissed the corner of her cheek. She gently wrapped what remained of her sandwich placing it in the seat on top of the folded brown bag. Then she grabbed the container of fruit closest to her. Nadene offered it up to the other two women before taking a deep red berry and putting in in her mouth. They ate in relative quiet. This was the first time in days that it was simply quiet. The room was still and the grey beyond the window was turning dark. As Alena chewed, she realized something when doing the math in her head. Alexandria had been only forty-eight hours in the past but that included the travel time.

"Nadene, how long were you passed out?"

"What?"

"When the chloroform knocked you out how long were you passed out?"

"Oh, a good number of hours. It was dawn, I think by the time we got out, and then a couple hours before the paramedics and the team showed up. Phone calls had to made as well. So, there was…" She thought about it again for a moment, "I guess about a good twenty-four hours between your kidnapping and my phone call."

"We were taken to France. We must have been dragged out shortly after we were knocked out."

"Yes, I remember getting hit on the back of my head." Alexandria remembered.

"Peter, must have had a plane on standby or something but Alexandria is only an hour ahead."

"What are you thinking?" Alexandria had a look of puzzlement on her face, trying to connect Alena's spoken thoughts.

"I don't know. I just feel like I am missing time."

"That's a very common feeling," A very masculine voice said from the doorway of the room. "Apologies, I didn't mean to startle anyone," the well-dressed man said, seeing their faces.

"And you are?" Nadene said as she casually popped another berry into her mouth.

"I am Jack Wills. I am the investigator assigned to your case. I was given a ring when the doctor saw that you were awake and eating."

"Oh," Alena shrunk a bit at the memories of a few hours before.

"I spoke to *you* earlier, didn't I?" Alexandria looked a bit closer at the well-dressed chap.

"Yes, you and I spoke, but I believe to get the full story I need to speak with Alena. If she is up for it." Mr. Wills nodded his head and gestured in a way on understanding. "So, Ms. Martin what do you say, do you remember anything?"

"Oh, I remember everything." Alena, being an officer of the law herself, knew to tell every bloody detail because even the slightest thing could mean something. She recounted everything she remembered, starting from when they went into the Library of Alexandria ruins until she woke up here. "I don't know how long I was asleep for, to be honest," She said, "That's the only time I can't account for."

"Well, you were out of surgery after several hours for the glass and bullet wounds, then recovering, and you slept for several hours after that." Jack Wills provided the answer the doctor gave him.

"Actually, that makes sense. As you heard, when you walked in, there was some time I couldn't recollect."

"Dear, you were asleep for some time. That is why it's been forty-eight hours since Alexandria. Longer than you thought and why you were so hungry when you woke up." Alexandria offered. She reached her hand to hold Alena, which Alena gratefully gripped. Alexandria hadn't left her side.

"Did you see what happened after your mother shot, this Mr. William Pritcherson?"

"No," Alena shook her head, refocused on the reasonably attractive detective, "Um, it gets really fuzzy after that, I remember grabbing my phone, leaning on mom," a shared glance passed between mother and daughter, "and then standing against the doorframe as she started and brought a car closer for me to get in, after that I don't know. I woke up here. I honestly thought I was going to bleed out in the car."

"If your mother had actually waited like she was told, you might have, but you didn't and you're here to live through it." He continued to write down in his little notepad. "Do you have any questions?"

"Yes, actually, um have you categorized all evidence?"

"No, we are missing your weapon that was discharged multiple times, it's evidence and it may be a murder weapon."

"Murder, those were flesh wounds that I shot into him, he should live. The last round might take some time to heal. But he should heal."

"Unfortunately, I must be the barer of ill news, William Pritcherson died." There were genuinely stunned looks across the women's faces.

"I didn't—I just—what am I supposed to do?" Alena Martin was the first to break the silence.

"Well, I don't think you killed him, there was massive trauma in his neck. I'll spare some details, but it obviously didn't match the others caliber of bullets within the rest of the crime scene. As you know the trajectory and the kind of bullet makes all the difference in determining defensive gunfire or the intent to kill." Jack Wills said.

"I swear I hate the man, especially after finding out what happened to my mother, but I would rather see him behind bars than dead." Alena said, looking at Nadene and Alexandria. "I didn't kill him."

"Don't panic, I believe you, but we need you to stay until we clear you. I think you fired a couple of defensive shots and left. I think there was a third party involved, personally."

"You mean, you think someone went in after we left and shot him, killing him and framing me?" Alena said in disbelief.

"Yes, do you have any enemies?"

"Yes, but none that would go to those lengths. Besides most of my enemies are already behind bars."

"High case-closure rate?" Jack Wills smiled admiring a fellow peace-keeper.

"Yea, something like that." She smiled back.

"I will get to the bottom of this. I don't think you did this. I have a working theory. I will find out who did, even if this is the last case, I take." Mr. Wills stated, meaning every syllable.

"Thanks," Alena smiled, "How do you know I didn't do it?"

"Well. There were shotgun pellets found at the scene and possibly two rounds filled the trauma in the neck."

"Well, that eliminates us, we used my hand gun." Alena said.

"Right, I am actually going to need to take that as evidence, anyway." Wills remembered.

"Oh, sure not a problem." Alena nodded to her mother who handed the weapon to the detective He pulled out an evidence bag and placed the gun in the bag.

"Thank you for being so cooperative, I'll get this back to you as soon as we run a few tests."

"Are we allowed to leave the country?" Alexandria asked.

"Umm, normally no, but is there a reason?"

"Well, it's a complicated family matter that needs tending in London."

"When we clear this up, I'll give you a ring? That's the best I can do right now." Jack Wills genuinely wanted to help but had to do his job here.

The women nodded their heads as he walked out of the door, placing the evidence bag in his coat pocket.

The Retaliation

Chapter XXVI

.... Two Weeks Later

Chapter XXVI

A blue sedan was driving up to the Benakis family estate. James Benakis had been released from the hospital late last week and arranged for Alena and Adara to visit. James was a bit slow and tired since returning home, but this visit was important. On their way home, his sister and niece decided it would be best to visit, since they were already in Europe. They had been released after they were cleared on all charges of the recent violence. All evidence had been proven in their favor, with a working theory being a set-up. Someone had attempted to frame Alena, but the obvious problem with the set-up working was the gun being different. After a number of tests being run, forensic analysis and several interviews, they were cleared. The vehicle approached the front of the mansion. It was parked under the carriage cover that was installed in the early 1800's and the car door was opened by the valet. He walked out of the house door for a proper greeting.

"Adara," He was nearly breathless with seeing her for the first time in thirty-five years. "You look great."

"I have aged, James, but thank you, it's great to see you too." She approached him with caution. She knew of his condition as they had spoken on the phone a few times since. His heart attack had taken a great deal of strength from him. James was to be limited in his activities until he regained it. But family was important. He embraced his sister, holding her in a way that he hoped she would never disappear again.   While holding her, a young woman got out of the car. Her heard was auburn, like burgundy with fire swirling in a crystal decanter, her skin fair with light freckles and piercing blue eyes. She wasn't thin but strong in her profile with soft edges, a round face. He was immediately reminded, in part of his youngest sister, especially around the eyes. The hair must have been from her father.

"You must be Alena." He released Adara and carefully walked to Alena. He hesitated, and she stuck out her hand as if he was to shake it.

"Alena, we are family. I am your Uncle James." He carefully embraced her. He could feel her cringe in his arms. "Oh, I am so sorry, I forgot, are you okay?" he said remembering her shoulder.

"I'll heal…It is good to meet you, James" She said as the tinge of pain slowly subsided. They stood there for a moment as the staff member at the door opened it to welcome them all in. Alena walked in with surprise.

"You never told me about this place,"

"I couldn't" Adara responded.

"How about some tea?"

"That sounds wonderful," Adara said as she walked in. She looked about the estate, "It hasn't changed at all."

"I tried very hard to keep it as such. Blanche and I had a restoration of the property about ten years back. I want you both to know, that I have an ulterior motive aside from simply tea."

"Oh?" Alena said.

"I am drawing up a will, just in case," The women looked at him in concern, "do not worry, doctors say I am fine, the hormone treatment is working. But I just want it to be clear that if anything should happen to me, my next of kin, you two, get this place."

"James, should it not go to your children," Alena said.

"My wife and I never had children"

"We—"

"I know, it's okay, especially now that I have finally found you," They walked through the halls towards a large open room, the parlor and music room. There was a piano in the eastern corner near a window, the walls were a pale green with the French doors at the far wall facing the group, a floral pattern on the molding in the ceiling. Victorian chairs and a small matching sofa sat in the middle of the room around a small coffee table. They approached the furniture when James started the conversation back up, "Tell me, Alena, how did you figure it out?"

"Um actually, it's a funny story, I didn't."

"I don't understand," James stopped just short of the table. Adara sat across from him. Alena sat beside her on the sofa, James sat after them on the chair across from them. "I don't understand then, how did you find everything out?"

"Well, that is a story to tell. But I didn't, truth be told, figure it out, it all unraveled for me." Alena started from the beginning and told her uncle everything. Starting with the phone call she got from him to the plane ride to Alexandria and what she remembered of her shared abduction with her mother. She had a few sips of tea, but she preferred hers with a touch of lemon rather than milk. Adara stayed quiet letting Alena recount the last several weeks to James. When she stopped her story in the hospital

Adara finished it. "That's when I called you, the truth was out and there was nothing left to hide. I told Alena after we had been cleared of the alleged charges."

James Benakis was silent, pondering. After a moment, he finally said, "That is why you left without a word all those years ago?"

"Yes,"

He didn't say his words in anger or fear but in sorrow, "Did you see Mariana before she—" he still couldn't bring himself to say the words.

"Yes, and I was at her funeral"

Surprise flooded his face, twenty-eight years ago she was there, she was so close. He was with her. "I didn't say anything because so much had changed and I wouldn't have known what to say to you. My husband carried Alena while we sat in the back row. I thought you would have given up on finding me."

"Never, I never gave up,"

"I can attest to that." Alena held up the file as she pulled it out of her messenger bag. The file was the same one that she had taken with her to Alexandria, Egypt. By the time she was taken, she had taken notes thinking maybe it had been a voluntary disappearance. However, until it was all actually revealed, she didn't understand the motives, the why.

"I see that now, and now we can be a family again."

"What do you both say to a walk in the gardens?"

"I'll just put the file on your desk, then shall I?"

"Please, I will tuck it away, safely later."

Adara looked at her older brother with kindness, "I think a walk on the ground would be wonderful." They put their tea down and walked out the glass French doors to the grounds of the estate. For the first time, in thirty-five years, James Benakis smiled as he looked at his sister.

***

The next afternoon, Adara and Alena were at the London airport waiting on their flight. Alena was finally able to put an old case to rest and now she could take the file back into work. This was a rare instance where pure circumstance solved the pieces. Her thoughts were interrupted when her phone rang, it was her friend.

"Stevie, how are things going?"

"Oh, good, hey your dog is fine, and everything is good here. The fire was finally contained, so that's good."

"Fire?"

"Yea, the fire, have you not seen the news?" Stevie replied in mild disbelief.

Alena realized she hadn't seen or even heard anything since she left LA. "I haven't exactly had time to catch a news station."

"It was nothing major, you know typical California fire season."

"Oh okay. Yea, that's great that they contained it. Was there any damage?" A sense of relief came over this news.

"Nothing more than during a normal fire season."

"Okay, great. So, What's up?" Alena asked not wanting to miss any flight updates.

"I was just checking on you. Oh, and last night, it's probably nothing, but I heard a noise in the house, it sounded like a door opening and then later closing."

"I don't understand, did you call it in?"

"No, I got up and checked the doors before I went to bed and locked everything. Nothing was missing or moved so I just thought maybe it was the air-conditioner being loud."

Alena chuckled, "Okay, we will look at it. You have no idea with this trip, we will have to go for sushi when I get back and feel up to it. Thanks for taking care of the rascal, we are on the way home can watch for one more night?"

"Yes, not a problem. We'll make a date for it."

"Thanks," She nodded her head as she hung up the phone.

"What was that about?" Alexandria inquired.

"Oh, it was just Stevie, she just wanted to check in."

"Gotcha, so how's the pup?"

"Good, didn't sound like any problems occurred or messes made." Alena really loved the pup, despite is crazy moments.

"That's good, I miss the little one."

"Me too."

"You know I was wondering, what do I call you now?" Genuinely curious, Alena asked the question aloud.

"What do you mean?"

"Well, is it Adara or Alexandria and do I call you Auntie?" Alena lightly laughed but was genuine in her question. But before she could speak the voice of a woman came on the speakers. Over the intercom system in the airport, their flight was being called for boarding. They grabbed their things, unplugged their devices and ensured that their tickets were out for easy access.

"What do you want to call me?" asked Adara as she walked side-by-side with Alena towards their flight's gate number.

"What I have always called you, what I know you by." Alena said a little unsure herself.

"Then that's what you call me," Adara said. Alena nodded as she cued in line to board behind her mother. Her phone vibrated in her back pocket. It was Nick.

"Hey, Nick!" Alena was actually surprised to get a call from him.

"Hi, um, I've been trying to call you?" Disappointment rang in his voice.

"Yea, sorry, I've been kinda busy."

"I figured but I wanted to ask you out on a date. I want more of a relationship."

"Nick, this isn't such a great time. A lot has happened that I need to focus on. You're a nice guy, but—"

"Okay, I get it, I can take a hint. I hope you find what you're after, I really do."

"Nick, it's been two dates." Alena stated, a little exasperated by his pressure for a relationship. Alena didn't want something serious right now, but Nick wouldn't let the subject go.

"I know, but some people know when they meet."

"Yes, and sometimes they don't and there is too much pressure to figure it out. I told you during our last date, Nick. I don't really want something serious right now. I don't have to see you every week for there to be a relationship. I want something build over time."

"I know—"

"Look, can we talk about this later, I have to catch a flight?"

"Yea, that's fine." Nick hung up the phone without saying good-bye"

Alena looked at her phone as the call ended.

"That was weird."

"What, trouble with Nick?" Alexandria asked.

"I don't know, nothing serious, I guess. We are on different pages and I shouldn't have engaged with him like that. What was I thinking?" Alena stated with mild confusion. "Go mom." The desk attendant was waving to scan Alexandria's plane ticket.

They put their carry-ons in the over-head bins and buckled up. For much of the flight Alena was asleep, head resting on Adara's shoulder. Adara stayed awake and read a popular book she had picked up in the shop in the airport. The flight was long and uninterrupted, there was the occasional conversation between mother and daughter. It had been the safest the pair had felt in some time, some thirty-thousand feet in the air. They landed in Los Angeles, twenty-four hours later, with a layover in New York and Kansas City. Nadene Jansen was there to pick them up from the airport and drive them the fifteen-minute drive to the house. Nadene had taken a flight two days beforehand, allowing her time to catch up with the time. They were welcomed home to the bark of Buddy, as Nadene helped the Martins into the beachside house. Collapsing on the couch, Alena noticed a piece of paper on the coffee table.

Stevie had left a note on top of the books on the coffee table. It was a short simple note:

I had to go catch up and do some work, I'll see you for sushi next week?

Xo Stevie

They were bombarded by the little dog. Alena cooed and grabbed the dog up, as he squirmed to run around the house. She placed him down and let him run, she picked up her bags with a wince in her shoulder and walked all of ten feet before Nadene stopped her.

"Hey, you know better, you could rip your stitches open."

"It's been two weeks." Alena said in defiance.

"Yes, but you never really let it heal, rest. Take a seat and take it easy. Those stitches come out in a couple more weeks, then you have physical therapy to deal with. You'll want your rest by then." Nadene took the luggage away from her and walked to the hallway. Alena's phone rang.

"Alena, I asked you to change that obnoxious X-Files ringtone a while ago."

"That's precisely why I kept it." She chuckled as she quickly opened the phone, recognizing the number.

"You're lucky, I have an international plan."

"Hello, to you to, did you arrive safely?"

"Yes, all quiet on the front." Alena smiled at the handsome, English voice on the other end of the phone.

"Good, um I just wanted to check and um…" he hesitated.

"Yes?"

"I am going to be in LA to finish up the details and give a personal copy of the file to your captain. I was wondering if I could take you to dinner" he paused "to clarify things and make sure I didn't miss anything."

"Uh-huh" she smiled at his lame excuse but took it anyway, "let me know when you are in town, Jack."

"Okay, I will. I am glad you're safe"

"TEA TIME!" she could hear her mother yell from the kitchen over the kettle.

"I have to go, find me on the messaging app so you don't rack up a bill," she chuckled "talk to you soon?"

"Absolutely, be safe." Jack Wills hung up as she put the phone down. Alena walked into the kitchen with Nadene who hugged her.

"I didn't give you a proper hug."

TEA TIME

"Thanks, but be careful of the arm." as Nadene released the light squeeze. They walked into the kitchen together with the dog at their feet. Alexandria had shaken the treat bag after putting the setting for tea on the table.

Chapter XXVII

…One Week later, Los Angeles 6:00 pm

Nadene walked into the kitchen of the house that the Martins had lived in ever since they came to Los Angeles some sixteen years ago. The leader of the house was definitely Buddy. The little black and white terrier bounded up to her with his friendly greeting. He was wearing a colorful little bow tie under his underbite. "Hi, sweet boy," as she picked him up, "I know, it's been a while since I have seen you."

"Nadene, it has been a week since you have been to the house," Alexandria smiled, "How's the dig? Have they found anything new since they have been cataloging everything?"

"A few scrolls and artifacts but they are still finding things, it is going to take us years to catalog everything. DNA tests, composition tests so much work to do, especially once they pull out Hypatia's urn next week." Nadene laughed, "This dig might rewrite history, we will only have to wait and see. I was going to touch base with Joey after dinner anyway, so I will let you know."

"Marvelous." Alena said from the kitchen.

"What have I told you about eavesdropping?"

"Make sure you time your entrance just so…?" Alena jokingly said as she walked back into the main living space.

"Fair enough, dinner—"

"Is ready, yes."

"Oh, I think I smell lemon. Alex you didn't make your famous potatoes?"

"I did, of course, with some help, as I had to make the salad and cook the lamb."

"We didn't have much else to do today to be honest," Alena said.

Nadene grabbed Alena, gently, "How are you healing? Physical therapy going well?"

"I got the stitches out yesterday so a little sore, but I am okay. I am heading back to work soon, so there is that, but I am considering a few things with all of this time. I had physical therapy later last week and another session today. If I didn't feel the injury to begin with, I certainly feel it now."

"She isn't sure if she wants to go back" Alexandria chimed in.

"That is not what I said, I am thinking of switching departments though"

"Oh, to where?"

"I haven't decided or discussed it really. Simply considering options."

"Well, whatever you put your hand to, I am sure you will succeed."

Alena smiled, "Thanks, we will see. But let's not have food get cold."

"Well, I am looking forward to it." Nadene smiled as she put the pup in her arms gently on the couch. What followed was a long overdue evening of good company and food. Each simply enjoyed the time spent together until a phone rang.

"Oh, it's mine, I'll be right back," Nadene said as she saw the caller ID. After a brief moment, Nadene walked back into the kitchen as Alexandria was clearing the table.

"Can you stay for desert?" Alena asked, handing a plate to her mother.

"I wish I could, but Joey found something, something big." Nadene said, she couldn't conceal her excitement.

"Bigger than Hypatia?" Alena asked. After dr. Jansen didn't respond she prodded, "What is it?"

"A door, with a message but no key, he can't identify the languages as they are a little worn."

"Pass them along if you have issues." Alexandria said.

"Of course, so I hate to do this, but I'll have to say good bye for the evening, I'll see you tomorrow?"

"Sure, maybe we can work on it together," Alena said, with only a glance to Alexandria, who simply nodded.

***

Nadene Jansen put the key in the door to her apartment. She used a small loft when she wasn't traveling or at a site but was teaching at UCLA. The key clicked, and the door moved inward just a bit. She had her teaching bag in her arms forcing her to lightly kick the door with her foot. Nadene put her bag down on a nearby chair and then flopped back on to the love seat a couple inches behind her. On a small table to the left of the love seat she placed her phone, her hand hitting the small Athena statue from her ex-husband on the table. The spear jabbed her.

"Ouch," she sat up and gripped her hand, her phone rang, "Damn, well, what did Joey want me to look at again?" she said aloud but to herself. She reached for the phone and remembered it was a message.

Check your email Dr.J said the message bubble at the top of her phone screen.

"Right," Dr. Nadene Jansen pulled out her laptop and booted it up. While she waited for it to load, she plugged in the device and went to the kitchenette for some water. A light chime sounded. It was her computer alerting her to proceed. She typed in her password and logged into her email.

"Okay, Joey, what did you find," she pulled out her reading glasses to get a better view as she zoomed in to the images that were uploading.

"The door—" the team had found this huge slab of a door in the chamber that was behind the first door, the porphyry purple door. The door that held Kendra and Sita captive. This door was different but the same in material as the other. Instead of being on ancient hinges like the first there was a riddle at eye-level and a key hole engraved into this one.

"Joey, what about the door," She rereads the email and then looks at the photo. But doesn't see anything, for a third time she reads the email and then blows the photo up and puts the email in a separate window. That's when she saw what he is talking about.

"Damn, I'm getting old." She shook her head and rubbed her eyes to look again at both image and email.

I don't recognize these dialects. I recognize the languages but there is a symbol in a couple of these lines that doesn't translate one way or the other and remains the same through the whole script. I don't know what it means, but I have a feeling it involves the key.

She looked closer at the images and the ever-observant Joey was right. There was a symbol here that she didn't recognize either. It looked like a combination of languages. If turned one direction it looked like something else than from another direction. Nadene pulled out her notes but didn't have any correlation between things, so with the limited ability she had she drew it out.

Nadene stared at it. That's when it dawned on her. It was in fact a symbol comprised of three long dead languages: Sumerian cuneiform, Egyptian Hieroglyphics, and the ancient Greek sun symbol of never-ending knowledge or truth. It said, with what she remembered from her limited ancient language studies, "To see the truth one must find the key." She wasn't sure what it meant but it was a broken sentence, there was context missing. She knew something was missing but she would have to find a way. "A key." That's what she wanted to start with.

Nadene Jansen was only starting on the theory when she heard a door close, ever so quietly. She wasn't alone. Without waiting or looking to find out she dialed 911.

"Hello, someone is in my apart—" she didn't get to finish the sentence. A masked man grabbed her from behind, he had been in the closet. Her phone fell out of her hand as she tried to remove his hand. He over powered her and threw her onto the couch, hand still on her mouth. He mockingly wagged is gloved finger, "tsk, tsk." He then grabbed the needle, filled with a chemical sleeping agent, out of his coat pocket. He uncovered the sterile needle and jabbed it into her neck as she persisted in her futile struggle. The drug took effect almost immediately. Her body betrayed her and went limp.

TEA TIME

The masked man placed Dr. Nadene Jansen onto the bed after lifting her from the couch. He placed her gently so as not to wake her or hurt her by hitting anything. He pulled out the phone in his pocket and tuned on the camera. He took a few photographs of the pages as they sat on her coffee table. There were sheets of symbols and codes, notes with added notes. She had started to work on a theory to discover the meaning of the multilingual symbol. Her laptop was open, still with her email inbox opened to the newest email from someone named Joey. He put his gloves on his hands and moved the pages so that he can read them. Taking photographs quickly of each page for his own resources. He shifted the pages back to the placement in the image to avoid anything being suspect.

Grabbing Dr. Jansen's phone, he dialed the number under the name Alexandria Martin. He let it ring, then heard a woman's voice answer, "Hello? Nadene, did you get home safe?"

***

Alexandria's phone rang. Alena heard it from the kitchen and walked to the living room where the phone was sitting on the table.

"Who is it?"

Alexandria reached for the phone. "That was fast, must have been no traffic."

"Well, answer her, mom."

She hit the swiped the green button on the screen and answered, "Hello? Nadene, did you get home safe?"

A man's voice came over the line, "You should keep your family closer and not hide or run from them."

"I'm sorry, who is this?" Alexandria questioned.

"We know each other," the voice said.

"Where is Nadene?"

"That's for you to find out…"

The concern began to build, but she kept it out of her voice, as she covered the phone against her chest, she mouthed 'call 911' to Alena who whispered for her to put it on speaker.

"Oh wonderful, I am glad you included Alena in this conversation," the man's voice said, it was deep and threatening. It sent a shiver down Alena's spine, the voice was familiar but couldn't place it.

"How is it we know each other…" the look of recognition was not lost on Alexandria but just another cause for concern.

"There is no point in calling the cops. I will leave you clues to find her, but it is Alena who needs to find her. I suppose you can come together, but there are things you both need to learn."

"Oh, like what?" Alena chimed in.

"Alena, have you reread your birthday letters recently, the ones your mother sent you?"

"What are you talking about?"

"There are clues, in the letters,"

"How do you know about the—" she realized something, "you were here."

"Very good, young lady." The voice was growing deeper with each word.

"Where is she, where is Nadene?" Alexandria nearly yelled.

"You will have to find her, but you are missing more than her. Have you ever wondered if your mother survived the gun fire of her would be assassin?"

"My mother died." Alena retorted.

"Did she?" the voice was playing with her.

"Why did she not come and find me then?"

"How do you know she didn't? How do you know she really isn't far from you, that she didn't watch you grow?"

"She would have sent some kind of sign."

"You're right, now if you're not careful you will have two bodies buried behind a door...come find them."

The line went dead. Alena stared at Alexandria. She couldn't breathe when the operator came back on the line. She snapped out of it long enough to give her badge number and the address of Nadene's apartment and assurance that she was on the way.

"What was he talking about, the letters?"

"The letter that I gave you each year, was in fact from your mother, my sister," she sat in a chair with a deep sigh. "They were hers, from her youth, but I had letters, every year on your birthday from a woman claiming to be your mother, I did not give them credence because I saw her get shot. I saw your mother die. The paramedics pronounced her dead after trying to save her life."

"Did you see her body? Afterwards?"

"It was an open casket funeral for both of them" Alexandria shook her head as she wrapped her mind about the possibility.

"Is it—is it possible that at least she survived but had to go undercover or something?"

"for nearly thirty years?"

"is it possible?"

"I suppose. Those are some extreme lengths."
Alexandria mused.

"Why? Why would she?" Alena mumbled to herself
as she grabbed her coat and walked beyond the couch.

"Alena do not go, you haven't fully recovered."
Alexandria pleaded.

"I have to go find Nadene, I can't lose what family I
have."

Alexandria nodded in understanding. She scratched
the ears of the dog as she walked past the couch. She didn't
say anything else, she put her arms around the young
woman she had raised, loved, and cared for as her own.

"Please, come back safely. Don't forget that
everything I have done was to keep you safe."

"I know,"

"I love you," she looked Alena straight in the eyes,
tears creeping up.

"I love you too. I will be careful, family first, no
matter what, remember?"

Alexandria nodded her head but held onto Alena for
a moment longer, then released. Alena, put her holster on,
then put her jacket on and walked out the door. Alexandria
heard the engine start and the sound dissipate. Then it was

all quiet. A few minutes had passed as she stared out the window. She fed Buddy his dinner. She picked up her tea from the kitchen table to wait with the dog for Alena to come back. After some time, she put the tea on the coffee table and dozed off on the couch in the living room, dog wrapped in her arms.

Alexandria woke up to the sound of a car in the driveway. She was too slow to realize that it wasn't Alena standing in the doorway. Alexandria reached for the bat underneath the couch. The masked man grabbed her arm and covered her mouth. He forced her to sit on the couch and held her down. A sharp prick was the last thing she felt as the horror sunk in and she went limp.

CPSIA information can be obtained
at www.ICGtesting.com
Printed in the USA
BVHW042207150919
558275BV00015B/238/P